A SCHEME BEYOND IMPERFECT

TARCIZO SOBREIRA FERNANDES

Library of Congress Control Number: 2025912056

ISBN
979-8-89641-076-8 (Paperback)
979-8-89641-077-5 (eBook)
979-8-89641-075-1 (Hardcover)

*To my wife, Marta,
my endless source of inspiration.*

A SCHEME
BEYOND
IMPERFECT

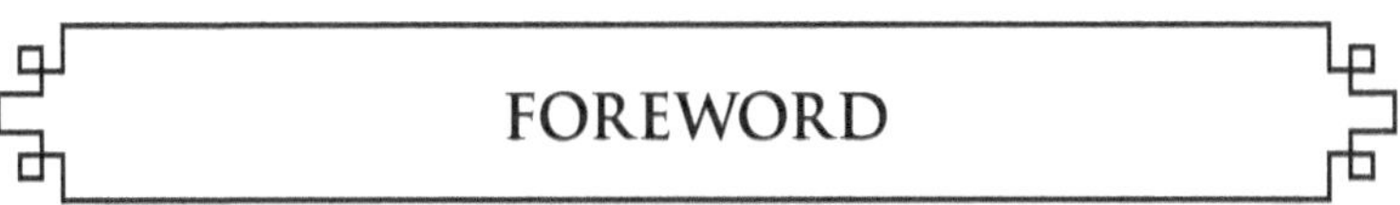

FOREWORD

When my friend and fellow retired naval officer Tarcizo Sobreira asked me to translate this book into English, I confess that I was reluctant to accept the task, mostly because I was swamped with other works for my editors. We then decided to discuss the matter over dinner in one of the dozens of restaurants that line the dazzling promenade of Copacabana Beach, in the city of lure that Rio de Janeiro really is. I therefore stocked myself with all kinds of excuses to decline without hurting my friend's feelings.

In his best elocutionary way, Sobreira summed up the meanders of a well hatched plot. Even before he got to the *grand finale*, I was absolutely convinced that the project would be a resounding bestseller, as it boasted all the trimmings to be made into a movie: suspense, romance, deception, drama, action, and murder. Furthermore, over and above all other factors and considerations, embedded in this tale of a search for a murdering terrorist is a story which exudes verisimilitude.

The characters, the descriptions, the behaviors, all are what one expects, and the subject matter is currently of the utmost interest. Sobreira succeeded in creating a fresh plot in this first-rate, dynamic tale with a terrifying "what if" at its heart.

Portugal and Brazil make up the setting for the events narrated herein. Inasmuch as Portuguese is the language spoken in those countries, the names of the characters had to be in accord with the author's original work. I thus decided not to Anglicize them in the wake of other well-accepted translations from French, German and Russian literature, where the personages get to keep their names unaltered.

I am grateful to Prof. Edward Thiery, my good friend Ed, for proofreading this book and also for his valuable advice while I was translating it. I have always been able to turn to him whenever a doubtful point arose in the idiom of Shakespeare, Dickens, and Twain, a language we both love ever so deeply. Without any false modesty, I must say I take pride in Ed's full recognition of the quality of my translation.

I voraciously read and reread this book before I sat down to translate it. It was written for those who appreciate the good writing that makes pleasant reading and have a mind open to possibilities no matter how dreadful they may sound.

So here it is, and I wish my friend Sobreira the best of luck with this magnificent endeavor in fictional prose.

–Antonio Martins Sepulveda,
Grapevine, Texas, 29 April 2011

INTRODUCTION

In April 2007, a major Brazilian newspaper published an extensive report on the actions of the Federal Police at a request from the American Central Intelligence Agency, regarding a thorough investigation into the activities of the "Moroccan Islamic Combatant Group" or "Moroccan Islamic Fighting Group," a Sunni Islamist terrorist organization affiliated with al-Qaeda, at the Triple Frontier in southern Brazil, through a terrorist who specialized in explosives and the martial arts.

This episode marked the first concrete sign of the infiltration of Islamic terrorism into South America.

In a tense narrative of continuous suspense, mixing fiction and reality with violence and emotion as strong ingredients, the author tells a feasible, topical story. He also details the preparation and subsequent execution of a terrorist's diabolical plan, working undercover as an instructor of martial arts at a gym in Brasilia, associated with one of his trainees, being both determined to cause a devastating impact on the media with unimaginable consequences.

A beautiful policewoman and her partner, a Portuguese detective from Lisbon, are given the task to seek out the terrorist's hiding place without being aware that the terrorist and his accomplice had devised a way to avail themselves of a unique moment to create havoc.

I take this opportunity to thank the people who invested so much of their time and effort into helping me put this book together, namely, Laerpe Motta, the celebrated artist responsible for the cover, Antonio Sepulveda, a fellow sailor who translated my work into the language of Melville, and also his lovely, talented daughter Karen Sepulveda Buls, whose attention to detail made the logistics of publishing possible. Finally, I wish to thank Sergio Pereira, my personal physician, whose valuable remarks and suggestions were quickly added to the text.

1

It was a little past seven in the morning in Brasilia, Brazil's capital. The intense sunshine on the horizon heralded a day of torrid heat. Young Ibrahim Hassan came rushing to the newsstand.

"Excuse me; you still got any copy of *The World* left?" he asked the vendor who was busy stacking up neat heaps of newspapers and magazines on the counter.

"Plenty. Here, take this one." The vendor whipped a copy off the top of the pile. "You're always up and around so early, and I…"

"Thanks!" Hassan cut him off snatching the paper with one hand, laying a few coins on the counter with the other, and then walking off without listening.

In a hasty stride he got to the small house where he lived, hurried inside, and slammed the door shut. He sat on the living room floor in a state of excitement. The stark expression on his face tersely denoted a grave concern as he spread out several newspaper sheets in front of him. He picked them out and perused the international news section. The headline glared up at him: "BAGHDAD: U.S. MISSILE HITS HOTEL KILLING 56." He began to read the story.

All of a sudden a deep chill ran through him, and his whole body quivered. That was the hotel where his mother, his grandmother, and his cousin and fiancée were supposed to be staying as far as he had been told. Hassan reread the article, masticating every word in the long hope that he might have misread it. The list of fatalities included Grandma Harwah, Tsouli, his mother, and Raissa, who was at once the cousin and fiancée with whom he was passionately in love.

"This can't be true!" he broke out into torrents of tears welling up in his eyes, flooding his cheeks and giving way to convulsive sobs that sounded somewhat like the suppressed roar of an enraged wild beast.

"Allah! Allah! Why such misery?" he cried rolling his eyes towards the ceiling. He sat there weeping for a long time, wiping his tears on his shirttail and sleeves, cursing and swearing, totally despaired.

Little by little, a sense of calm kicked in, but it was warded off with expletives followed by anguished wails, breaking up the silence of the room in a scene of endless sorrow devoid of any vestige of hope.

The afternoon was over. He got back on his feet, exhausted, and tottered over into his mother's room. He threw his six-foot-two, muscle-bound body on the bed, and it was sheer luck that kept it from caving in. Notwithstanding the puffiness in his face caused by swollen eyes from all that crying, Hassan, a Brazilian-born son of Iraqis, preserved his good looks. The dark complexion and an aquiline nose played up his Arab descent.

Still sobbing, he turned his thoughts to the eve of the women's journey to Baghdad, when he owned up his misgivings to his mother:

"Mother, I still don't like this trip you're taking with Raissa."

"Rubbish, dear. After we find your grandmother, we will hop on the first flight back. She wrote to ask for someone to pick her up, because she cannot travel alone. Also, she is in pain, mourning your grandfather who was labeled as an informant for the Americans and hence murdered by the terrorists."

From the day of their departure, Hassan took to buying the newspaper every morning, and, only after reading the latest news about the war in Iraq, he got ready and went off to work at the Presidential Palace where he was part of a top select group of handpicked military and civilian personnel thoroughly trained to be members of the President's personal security detail. In fact, he got that job almost by chance. Inasmuch as he was an expert in light weapons and highly-proficient in freestyle fighting, a skill he had acquired in his spare time when he was still mopping up floors at the Olympic Academy of Martial Arts, when Hassan later joined the Army he was immediately scouted out by Major William Blake who appointed him as his orderly. Upon his promotion to lieutenant colonel, Blake was picked to head the President's security guard. He sent for Hassan:

"Hassan, I've just been assigned to serve in the Presidential Palace. You're coming with me," he ordered, curt in manner and speech.

"Yes sir!" Hassan gave the only appropriate military answer under the circumstances.

Two months later, Ibrahim Hassan made the non-commissioned rank of corporal, and by intervention of his boss he was set apart for a position in the President's personal security detail. He was supposed to escort the President on every trip. He wore no uniform and earned a salary stuffed with fat incentives, not to mention hanging around with the country's highest authorities. There was only one snag: Hassan was an introvert, too shy and too quiet. He made friends with nobody. "A misanthrope," said the chief diplomat in charge of official ceremonies and protocol. "The Arab," as he had been dubbed, "seems more like a primitive brute," needled Homero, one of his fellow agents corroded by the envy induced by the notion of Hassan being the boss's pet. "He's a weird bird," added Fernandez, another agent. "His mind is focused on his fiancée, with whom he appears to be obsessed."

Still steeped in memories, Hassan suddenly stumbled upon the question of how he would live without a single member of his small family, all by himself. A man absolutely alone and unrelated to any other person in the universe. In view of his emotional fragility, he was a strong candidate for deep depression, just one step away from suicide. The setting of his emotions was invaded by an intense and inexplicable fear. His self-confidence was shattered by an avalanche of contradictory thoughts and the sudden foreboding of a lonely future. He was terrified.

Alone in his mother's room, he spoke broodingly:

"Without you, Mom, and without you, Raissa, my great love, I see no reason to continue living."

He sat up in bed and looked at the frame on the bedside table, which contained a picture of mother and fiancée, embracing and smiling.

Disturbing questions flashed like bolts of lightning in the background of his brain:

"So, they died for nothing? I lost my precious, dearly loved ones, and that's it? Isn't there a murderer? A culprit? What is happening here? Get out there, boy! Avenge your flesh and blood and your dearly beloved!"

The rush of adrenaline into the bloodstream was fiercely coursing through him. Hassan got up as though he had been sitting on a wasp's nest. He cried out:

"Damn! I almost forgot. There is a culprit, to be sure. Of course there is! He must die. I'll kill him. Then I'll kill myself."

Looking back at the frame he said loudly:

"I'll kill myself! Do you hear? My life no longer has a meaning, but I swear to you both that the world will be aghast at my revenge!"

He let himself fall back on the bed and rolled from side to side until daybreak, caught up in a whirlwind of memories and an ever-increasing hatred of infidels, a term used in the mosque to dub unbelievers with respect to Islam.

Hassan was still disoriented when he got up very early in the morning. He left the house in complete disarray, doors unlocked and lights on, and walked the streets totally oblivious to the world around him. Thus he roamed about in misery aimlessly all day long, wandering off, farther and farther away from his home. Night was upon him when he realized he was on the outermost, deserted corner of Lake Paranoa, a freakish place, shrouded in darkness and cloaked in a silence broken only by the constant rustle of the small waves brought on by the wind that blew over that large body of fresh water. He saw a low ridge over yonder. He climbed it easily and lay down on his back. As he looked up, he scanned a myriad of bright spots embedded in the huge dark cape that warmly covered the city with a lovely starry sky. Hassan took a deep breath in an attempt to relax. He felt calmer— actually, he was all in— and ready to work out a plan for vengeance to be carried out before putting an end to his own life.

Hassan gradually found some relief as he dipped into pleasant recollections that eased down the hate shown on his face. He remembered the day when he was sweeping up a barracks room, as Major William Blake came in and hugged his boss at the time, Major Silveira. Their conversation came back to Hassan:

"I'm here to relieve you. You can now make it back down home," Blake jested with a broad smile.

Silveira returned the hug.

"Thank God you're here. I really miss my tribe back in Rio."

"You mean your family aren't here in Brasilia?"

"How could they? We're talking five offspring here. Three of them in college. The girl is a journalist in a TV network. The youngest is preparing for the Scholastic Aptitude Test. I only get to see them every other week."

"Well, my friend, we go back a long way. In two days, you'll become a free man. I'll assume your duties, and you're off to Rio," Blake said with a contented grin.

"No doubt about that with your being the class genius and all. I'm sure you'll have no problem learning all there is to know about this billet in a couple of days."

The remembrance of that occasion vanished as Hassan, while still staring up at the sky, was distracted by a bright, non-twinkling, reddish dot of light. It was Mars, but he would not know that.

Suddenly, out of the blue, he recalled a most unusual experience. Two weeks after he had been Blake's orderly, Hassan was mustered to bear a hand unloading the moving van into the major's assigned apartment. Upon crossing the front door, he was met by a little boy, nearly three years old, a lovely, cherubic child who went by the nickname of Guto. He was Major Blake's and his wife Leticia's only child. Without the slightest hesitation, Guto ran into Hassan's arms, found the way up to his lap, neck, and shoulders, and from then on out nobody could get him off during the entire afternoon. The recollection came very clearly to his mind of the stunned look on his face that day: he just sat with that kid all along, while movers, fellow soldiers, the maid, the missis and the major carried heavy pieces of furniture back and forth. All he did was to hang around with Guto attached to his neck.

Hassan smiled. He remembered when Dona Leticia ran out of sitters to look after Guto. Hassan introduced his mother to the boss's wife, and Dona Tsouli went to work for the Blakes.

He and Raissa set the wedding day. His mother returned home, because she needed to work on a trousseau for her niece and future daughter-in-law. Hassan's multiple duties and the new job description of the newly-promoted lieutenant colonel caused the wedding to be postponed three times. The final date agreed would be by the end of that year, but this terrible tragedy befell them, and all their dreams were violently crashed, like a small boat in a rough sea.

Hassan resumed his crying.

It was dawn. A lull settled over that low ridge and kept him company. Still with his eyes on the stars and his thoughts in the past, Hassan reminisced about his mother telling him and Raissa the story of how they had ended up in Brazil after they fled the war that was about to break out between Iraq and Iran that began in September, 1980, and lasted until August, 1988.] They arrived in Brazil through Sao Paulo; her husband, her sister and her brother-in-law. Advised by an old Arab resident who had lived there for over thirty years, they went out West to settle down in Brasilia, where job opportunities in civil construction were aplenty and manpower was in higher demand than ever. In spite of the language barrier, husband and brother-in-law managed to be hired on for the construction of the only mosque ever erected in Brasília.

Her brother-in-law was a sickly and feeble man. When his wife died giving birth to Raissa, he allegedly died from grief a few months later.

Her husband, Hassan's father, on his turn was a hard-working man. With permission from the foreman, he methodically, every day, hauled small amounts leftover scraps, bricks and roof tiles from the mosque construction site over to a small piece of land he had purchased with the savings amassed from years of working 80-hour weeks back in Iraq. He built their small house piece by piece, but he never suspected the real reason the foreman allowed him to take that material was a mere diversion, because the foreman himself made off with large quantities of it himself. Had the foreman been caught, he would have put the blame on Hassan's father. Nevertheless, nobody ever noticed or found out anything.

Though professing Islam, the father tended to overlook the fact that liquor was off limits to Mohammedans, for he indulged in heavy drinking spouts. One day at lunch break, while celebrating the birth of his son Ibrahim, he had one too many, lost his balance, and fell down an open elevator shaft, breaking his neck.

Hassan and his cousin were raised by Dona Tsouli who suddenly saw herself as the washerwoman employed to launder clothes and linens for middle-class families. Those were the meager days, the lean years.

Things began to look up when he and Raissa were enrolled in a public school on the outskirts of the city. They could learn and play with other children, and, to a degree deserving of special emphasis, they were fed rice and beans and, from time to time, a soy steak.

Those were easier days, the lighter years.

Hassan smiled when he remembered how in those days, at less than eighteen years old, he found himself in love with Raissa; and she with him. Shortly thereafter, she went to work in a daycare center. He got a job as janitor at a martial arts academy where one could learn the best of *tae kwon do*, karate, judo, jujitsu, and wrestling. Big and strong as he was, he made some extra cash by offering himself as a sparring partner for the fighters and wrestlers in training. Hassan was young and quick to perceive and apprehend the traits and mannerisms of each style. He learned fast and even created some new moves. At night he went to school. Learning was no problem to him as he was one of the top students in his class. By the time Hassan was preparing for the entrance exams to get into college to get a degree in physical education, the Army had not filled its draft quota for that year, and he was included in the number of inductees that were to be selected by the draft board to be sent to a boot camp. Bursting with health, he was the first to be inducted. There would be no more tips to increase his income, and his standard of living lowered to the level of bare subsistence. He gave all his wages to his mother and wore his uniform everywhere to save his civilian clothes.

At daybreak, the negative urge for vengeance came back to his mind. He would never turn away from the straight, prescribed course of revenge for the murder of his family.

In his mind the person to answer for the annihilation of his kindred had to be an American. The ideal choice would be the imbecilic pilot of that fateful bomber, but that option was immediately ruled out; it would never happen, because it was impossible to find out who he was. Killing a random American did not make any sense, since it would accomplish nothing; it would be sheer stupidity. His best choice would have to be a high- ranking person of great importance and influence, a dignitary who commanded special treatment; someone whose assassination might be capable of igniting public outrage, protests and a fueled international outcry. The U.S. ambassador to Brazil somehow fitted the description; he was close by, within reach, and he paid frequent visits to the Presidential Palace.

Hassan sprang up to his feet, beat off the sand that was strewn to his clothing, and cried out loud in sheer delight:

"Unless fate has it that I may come up with a better name, which I very much doubt, this Gringo is my target. Then I'll blow my brains out."

The morning was far along when Hassan returned home feeling like trash.

Revealed by the first rays of the sun his appearance was frightening. Dirty, unshaven, with huge dark circles under the eyes, Hassan looked like a down-and-out, homeless beggar. As he stared at his eerie reflection in the mirror, he made a most simple decision: to resume his life as usual. He would act as though he had completely overcome the appalling emotional shock that had actually created a substantial, lasting damage to his psyche. He decided that nobody could entertain the slightest suspicion of his intentions. Hassan's job requirements kept him under the lens of constant scrutiny as to his behavior, friendships, words spoken, places visited, and opinions issued on political figures or their kin. Everything was closely weighed in and carefully pondered on. Inasmuch as he was planning on perpetrating a folly, he would have to be very careful not to lose his chance. He shaved, showered, donned his best suit and tie, and headed off to the Presidential Palace, knowing exactly what he had to do. He thought to himself: "I'm going to explain to the colonel why I missed a work day for the first time in my entire life. And then, ever so calmly, seriously keeping my cool, I'll carry out my plan."

Ibrahim Hassan could never have imagined, at that moment, that his plan to kill the U.S. ambassador to Brazil and then commit suicide was to undergo a U-turn that would lead to a most extraordinary event. It would go down in history and never be forgotten.

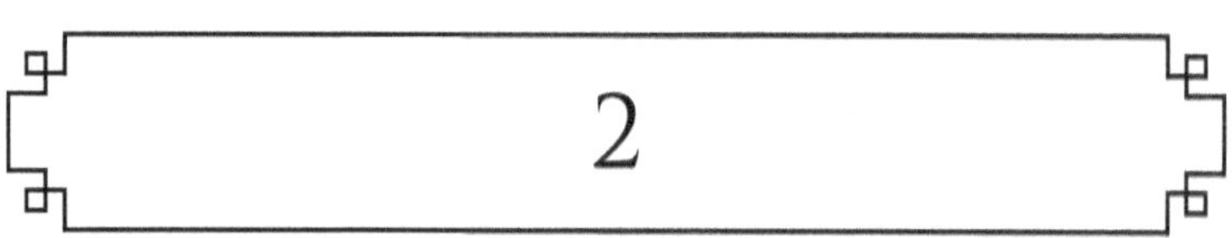

2

Fair skin, green eyes, medium height, Lieutenant Colonel William da Silva Blake hailed from Manaus, a city in west central Amazonia and the capital of Brazil's northern State of Amazonas, smack in the heart of the largest rain forest in the world. He was the only child of an American father and a Portuguese mother. His parents met, got married, and lived in Brazil.

After graduating at the top of his class from the Brazilian Military Academy, working his way through a brilliant career, he was meritoriously granted a tour of duty as the Brazilian exchange officer at the United States Army War College in Carlisle, Pennsylvania. Upon returning he was transferred out to Brasilia. He had then the rank of major. In less than a year, already a lieutenant colonel, Blake was appointed to command the president's security guard. He reported for duty accompanied by his former orderly Ibrahim Hassan, now to become a member of his team.

That morning, Blake was summoned by the minister in charge of the General Intelligence Agency (GIA), Lucio Fanzine. The colonel was ordered to coordinate the security agents on a two-day trip that President Felipe Ferraro was to make to Argentina, one of the four member countries of the Southern Cone Common Market, known as Mercosur.

"None of my business, sir, but what's the real reason for the trip this time around?" Blake asked with a smoldering cigarette in one hand and a memo in the other.

"Don't know yet for sure. Maybe it has something to do with some sort of complaint from one of the partners or..."

The minister was interrupted by the interphone.

"Yes, Dona Celia," the minister answered, tapping the ash of the cigarillo into the ashtray."Yes. OK."

He shut off the interphone and said to Blake: "One of your men, agent Carlos, is outside. His business appears to be compelling."

Blake excused himself and left the room.

"This had better be really important!" he said upfront when he saw Carlos standing by Celia's desk with arms folded.

"When I'm in there," the colonel added, pointing to the door to the chief's room. "I hate to be disturbed."

"Good morning, colonel," Carlos replied in a tone of reproach for not having heard at least a simple greeting from him.

"Well, sir," Carlos went on, "Ibrahim Hassan was reported absent at roll call this morning when I was supposed to muster those who have been selected to join the security team on the president's upcoming trip. He hasn't shown up yet."

"My orderly?"

"That's right, Sir."

"Did you give him a buzz?"

"By all manners of means. His cellphone is out of the service area, and no one is picking up the phone at his place. I sent a man over. There was nobody home, although doors and windows were wide open. All very weird."

Blake ran a hand over one of his eyebrows, a nervous tick that signaled apprehension and concern.

"Strange," he muttered,"very strange. Hassan never pulled a stunt like that."

"As the staff is already being briefed for this mission," Carlos said,"I told Viegas to take his place."

"You did well," said Blake."Are you scheduled to go, too?"

"No, Sir. I'm staying. Don't worry! I'll personally find out why he is missing and keep you posted."

"Yeah, OK! Do that!" Blake concurred.

Colonel Blake was frowning in displeasure as he walked back into the chief's office, closing the door behind him.

Lt. Col. William Blake's wife, Leticia, was a psychological pedagogue who taught developmentally challenged children at Santa Cecilia School. A charitable woman, every other week she spent the afternoon at the St. Louis Orphanage run by nuns, teaching forty homeless children to read and write.

Hassan's house was on the way, so Leticia was in the habit of stopping by for a quick visit with Tsouli. That afternoon, somewhat distracted, she pulled up on the driveway and rang the doorbell. Nobody answered. That was when she remembered her friend had traveled to Iraq. She found it very strange that the doors and windows were open. She went in. The house was a total mess; newspapers all over the floor. That was not like Tsouli or Hassan. They were both very efficient, methodical, and tidy. Leticia was very fond of them, because they were both so attached to her son Augusto, her little Guto.

Leticia got back in the car and drove on to the orphanage. For some reason she could not get off her mind the fondness that existed between the child and the former orderly. It was touching to watch that sturdy soldier play as if he were the same age as Guto, rolling on the floor, crawling on hands and knees to be the boy's horsy or playing hide-and-seek. Sometimes Guto would pull Hassan's hair and pinch his nose; in short, the dour, reticent, extremely reserved Bahim, as the boy had dubbed him, would come tumbling down in front of that pipsqueak. Their friendship never wavered for a moment. One day Leticia heard Tsouli say, "There is only one creature in this world capable of doing whatever he pleases to my son, which includes making him laugh, and that's your boy, little Guto."

"That's true. My son is immensely fond of that sullen-faced Arab." Leticia had agreed with a smile.

Still in the car on the orphanage's parking lot, she called her husband's mobile."No service," she thought. "He must've left on that trip to Argentina."

She then decided to call the colonel's secretary. No answer. Leticia was almost giving up, but she remembered to try the secretary of the minister.

"General Fanzine's office. How can I help you?" the secretary answered.

"Celia?"

"Yes. Who is this?"

"This is Leticia Blake."

"Oh, Dona Leticia! Sorry I didn't recognize your voice."

"No problem, my dear. Can you tell me whether Ibrahim Hassan went with my husband on this trip?"

"No, ma'am, he didn't. And the colonel was very much worried when Agent Carlos told him that Hassan was absent without leave."

In Buenos Aires, the summit of presidents of Mercosur countries was drawing to a close.

Suddenly, Colonel Blake felt the vibration of the cell phone in his pants pocket. Quietly, lest he should interfere in the speech of President Felipe, he walked to the opposite side of the room and, hiding behind a column, he cupped the phone with the left hand. "Yes!" he whispered.

"Colonel?" the metallic voice was Carlos's.

"This is Blake!" Blake had toned his voice down to a murmur.

"Hassan is back! He hasn't reported to me yet, but I know he is in the Palace. Can you hear me, colonel? Everything is OK. No need to worry."

"Alright! I hear you. Hassan has shown up and all is well. Thanks! I'm hanging up."

Walking as silently as a cat, Blake went back to his post behind the president's seat, where he stood and kept his eyes on every corner of the room, watching and listening for the slightest movement in the audience.

As security agents scattered in a crowd can communicate in code through subtle, deceptive gestures, imperceptible to the layman's eye, it didn't take long for the colonel to let the whole team in on the Arab's reappearance. All's well that ends well.

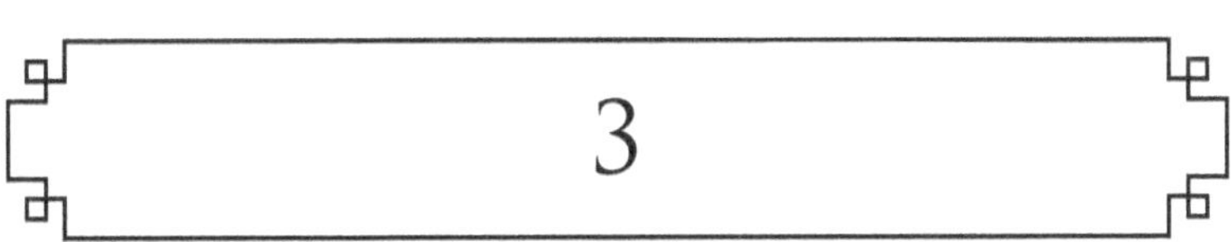

3

After making friends with the president, Luiza, the widow of Congressman Mauricio Prado, ended up marrying Felipe Ferraro. She proved not only to be a good wife and a great chum, but also a fantastic lady.

Luiza had refined habits and taste. She had been born into a traditional and highly respectable family from Oporto, a city of northwest Portugal near the mouth of the Douro River north of Lisbon. Insightful and unwavering, she was a clever and discreet counselor who knew how to comport herself quite effectively behind the scenes within the high circles of the civilian and military hierarchies.

Thanks to her competent counsel and guidance, President Felipe Ferraro made many a sound decision which increased his popularity.

Ferraro scored a great success when, under Luiza's guidance, he managed to minimize the pressure from the large majority of oil-producing countries against the gradual replacement of the black gold with other sources of energy. She convinced the Minister of Foreign Affairs to convey to his counterparts the suggestion of following in the wake of Brazil and start producing other types of fuel. It was a scenario where everyone would benefit, not necessarily through someone else's loss. New internationally-funded research programs would be developed in a pool of cooperation thus bringing pollution down to acceptable limits. The agreements addressed the concurrence of Brazil, the United States, and other countries from Europe, the Middle East, Africa, and the Americas in the measures regarding a cooperation that would be offset by a significant decrement of agricultural subsidies and taxes according to rates supposedly advantageous to the most resourceful members. Indeed, over the medium term, the rich countries would derive more benefits. Inasmuch as by definition globalization is a dynamic process, the growth of emerging countries would be faster, thereby improving their standings with the benefits from research projects, new jobs, stimulated industry, and the overall development that would push them upwards a bit closer to the wealthy nations, although the gap, when all was said and done, would still remain quite noteworthy. This may sound like a somewhat utopian scheme for parceling out wealth, but in the long run nobody would really lose, and the planet would be most grateful for the reduction of greenhouse gases. To cap the celebration of the agreements, Brazilian diplomacy envisioned a grand ceremony aboard the aircraft carrier Rio de Janeiro, laying at anchor in Guanabara Bay. The leaders of the nations involved would gather on the flight deck for the signatures and, immediately afterwards, they would all indulge in a large variety of Brazilian dishes served at a fellowship gourmet luncheon on the flattop. Needless to say that an event of this level on board a warship would have to be safe. The aim was to enact something similar, but more expressive than the usual G-20 summits.

After several meetings of ambassadors, ministers and various highly skilled adepts, they had managed to secure approval from their respective governments. The ceremonial event was scheduled to take place on October 15th, after all participants confirmed attendance. It was April, so they had seven months left to wrap up preparations.

It was agreed that the planning for the event would be kept in secrecy to avoid premature speculation, criticism, and negative political reactions.

4

The presidential security agent, Ibrahim Hassan, reported to Agent Carlos.

Although he understood the situation and truly commiserated with Hassan over the pitiful loss of his whole family, Carlos could not hide his vexation at not having been informed that the tragedy that had made all the headlines involved one of the president's body guards. Neither he nor anyone else knew anything about such a heart-rending fate. He dissimulated his cast of mind, sought to conceal it from Hassan, and lied through his teeth, saying that the colonel was greatly dismayed by the news and understood perfectly his absence from work. Hassan pretended to believe him.

"Let's wait for the colonel!" Carlos said. "Arrangements shall be made for the recovery of the bodies. Meanwhile go on leave for a few days. Take an even strain! Why don't you go home and try to get some sleep?"

"No, sir. I prefer to go back to work. It'll make the pain a bit more bearable." He pulled out his handkerchief and wiped a tear born out of an intense mental state that arises subjectively rather than through conscious effort. "No leave," Hassan added. "I'm going back to my desk." He turned his back and walked away.

Carlos reached for the phone and dialed a number.

"Colonel?"

"Speaking."

"This is Carlos. Hassan is back at his desk. He's waiting for you.

"We'll be landing this afternoon at about half past three."

It was nearly five o'clock p.m. when Blake arrived at his office and sent for his former orderly on the double.

"Please allow me to express my profound sorrow and deepest condolences for the terrible tragedy that has struck your beloved family," he said getting up and, with both his hands, grasping Hassan's right hand.

Hassan pulled a long sigh.

"Thank you, boss!" he said, standing at attention and squeezing the colonel's hand. "It's a tough break, but I'm dealing with it."

"I will personally contact the Iraqi authorities through the Foreign Ministry and request that the bodies be identified and flown home." said an apologetic Blake.

After a few seconds of silently staring at the colonel, Hassan said:

"I appreciate your kindness, sir, but asking for identification and transfer of the bodies is sheer waste of time, as you will agree. I've read all about it in the papers. The hotel was blown up and burned out. That missile left a crater 120 feet wide and 30 feet deep and smashed up everything within a radius of 300 yards. There is nothing to recognize; much less identify."

Hassan cleared his throat before he went on.

"That place is hell. There is no way of knowing who used to be who. There are no technologies nor the means to sort things out. Again, I am most thankful to you, Colonel. This misfortune is now part of the past. I am determined to bury that past and carry on with my life. My work will help me in this endeavor. May I be excused now, sir?" Blake nodded. He could barely believe what he had just heard.

Hassan did an about-face and left the room, quietly closing the door behind him.

Blake was stunned, dumbfounded, totally taken aback at the soldier's rhetoric.

"This can't be for real!" he mused. "He must've had that speech memorized down to the last word. That wasn't like him at all. I thought I knew Hassan better than himself? He is usually so monosyllabic. I never imagined that he could ever express himself like that. Could it be that his untalkative ways are some sort of gimmick? To what purpose?"

At the end of office hours, Hassan hopped on the motorcycle and raced back to his home. After changing into Bermuda shorts and a T-shirt, he sat on the porch steps, facing the garden.

Once more he plunged down memory lane. It started out with a sudden, unexpected recollection of Raissa working at the orphanage managed by The Children's Paradise, a non-governmental organization in the nearby town of Taguatinga. It was one of his most moving experiences. Hassan was sitting on a bench at a small playground where some children tended by his fiancée were at play. A small blond boy with the bluest eyes that he had ever seen came up to him, hugged his legs and asked: "You want me for you? Wanna be my daddy?"

Hassan would never forget that scene. He would never get over the piercing emotion of that moment. But there was more.

He picked up that little angel and put him on his lap. "Take me wid ya," the boy whined.

That did it. The remembrance of that day made him break into tears for the umpteenth time. Engulfed with an overwhelming sense of emptiness, he glared up at the heavens and sent forth a message with his husky, grating voice: "No sweat, my love! We'll soon be together in Paradise. Just be a little patient. First, I need to send a major-league Gringo to the abode of devils and condemned souls."

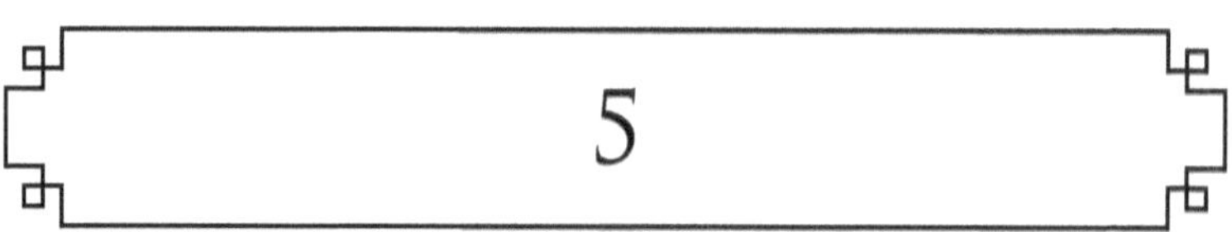

5

There are about one billion and seven hundred million Muslims in the world, and its population is increasing at 1.84 percent per year. Gamal Abdul was one of them. He was part of a sect made up of fundamentalist radicals and belonged to a terrorist cell group of Iraqi Islamists linked to al Qaeda. Gamal had a way with languages; he could learn them effortlessly. After spending a few years in Macao before it came under Chinese control in 1999, he acquired a very good command of Portuguese. After working a while in that overseas province, he was ordered off to Portugal to learn how to cook, starting out as a kitchen helper. Upon graduation he would head across the ocean to Brazil. He was mailed an envelope with coded instructions and a cashier's check.

In Lisbon, he stayed in a hostel in Bairro da Graça, where he became friends with Eduardo Santana, a student from Braga, a city of northwest Portugal north-northeast of Oporto.

"Why don't you do your cooking in France," Eduardo asked him, "where the food enjoys a much higher reputation?"

"Two reasons," Gamal replied. "First, there's the language barrier. I don't speak a word of French and I sure can't take time to learn. Second: there is greater affinity between the cuisine here and in Brazil. "

"Going to Brazil?"

"Right! I'm fixing to become a chef in a Brazilian restaurant."

"Never been to Brazil," said Eduardo. "One of my brothers spent some time out there, and he grew very fond of the place."

"You got many brothers?" Gamal asked.

— There are five of us, and we're all confirmed, old bachelors. On the last Saturday of each month, we get together and have lunch with our folks in Braga. We have a reunion coming up the day after tomorrow. Would you like to tag along and see Braga? The chow is just divine! We'll be back in Lisbon on Sunday.

"No, thanks! I have to go about my life. I need to mosey around and try to find out where I can learn to prepare sophisticated dishes."

On the following Tuesday, back at the hostel, as Gamal was engaged in chat with Eduardo, he fumbled around with his open suitcase on an armchair and accidentally dropped a small bag out of which a flask came rolling across the floor, and a sheet of paper with drawings of symbols and slogans written in Arabic landed at Eduardo's feet.

"What do we have here?" Eduardo said, picking up the paper.

Gamal seized it back hastily from his hands and grabbed the flask.

"My stuff. Things to remember my homeland by," he uttered lamely in a visible state of sudden, overpowering panic.

"Funny, I think I saw a little bottle once that looked exactly like that one and also some scribbles with a similar depiction," Eduardo said, frowning and pointing at the terrorist's hands. Let me try to remember. On TV? Some magazine? Newspaper? The Internet, of course. That's it! I'll pull it up and show it to you tomorrow."

Gamal locked up his suitcase and left the hostel without saying a word. He returned at two in the morning. Everyone was sound asleep, and all was quiet. Sliding through the dormitory like a shadow, he leaned over Eduardo's bunk. Expeditiously and with professional skill, he used a pillow and a sharp-edged razor to smother his friend's face and slit his throat. Eduardo was dead in a matter of seconds. Gamal covered the corpse with a blanket, grabbed his suitcase and left the building without a noise. Very early in the morning he was on a TAP plane on his way to Brazil. By the time they found the bloody body of his victim, Gamal was halfway across the Atlantic Ocean.

Eduardo's older brother was Inspector Mauricio Santana of Interpol office in Lisbon. He had traveled the day before to Angola in pursuit of a counterfeiter of euro banknotes.

Upon arriving in Sao Paulo, Gamal checked into a hotel near downtown. He spent three days there. Then he headed south towards the small town of Iasci on the so-called Triple Frontier, the border area where Argentina, Brazil and Paraguay meet; it is an active South American center for contraband, drug trafficking, and money laundering; also a suspected locale for Islamic extremist groups. While there he was joined by two abettors. A few days later Gamal went off to Brasilia, where he took a practical test for admittance into the Olympic Academy of Martial Arts, and he was hired as a wrestling instructor. He became quite proficient in fighting skills during the two years he had spent in Milan. He took lodging in the Bajara Hotel, a rundown joint on a vicinal road that might come in handy in case he had to make a run for it. He could easily pass himself off as just a plain, average visiting foreigner if nobody ever found out the true meaning of the flask containing orange extract, a set of white clothes and a prayer on a sheet of paper, which were mandatory items for the ritual to be religiously performed by suicide bombers before they carry out their fatal attacks. That letter and that flask had already caused the assassination of an innocent student in Lisbon.

The prayer in Arabic was a profession of faith, the ultimate source of his will, and a farewell statement. Gamal Abdul was a most dangerous fanatical terrorist and held a high standing among his peers who were gradually infiltrating select countries in South America. His Arabian countenance drew the attention of Hassan who still paid night visits to the gym to work out and keep his fighting skills up to par. This practice also helped him fight boredom and kill time while waiting for the right moment to fulfill his vengeance.

Monday evening he left work early and went to pray at the mosque. He ran into Gamal.

"I'm surprised to see you here. I've never seen you talking to anybody around the gym," said Gamal in fluent Arabic, enunciating every word.

Well schooled from experience, Hassan preferred to maintain the utmost discretion in speaking with strangers, accordingly complying with the Security Agent Manual. But he did not want to be rude. His answer was terse: "You're right. That's the way I am. Excuse me." He walked off, climbed on his motorcycle, cranked it up and sped away.

Also an experienced man, well-versed in that walk of life and accustomed to dealing with most unusual personalities, circumstances and situations, Gamal stood there as he watched Hassan ride off, and spoke softly to himself in Portuguese with hardly any accent at all: "This guy has serious problems, and he probably suffers from a brutal psychological depression."

He looked up at the sky and thanked Allah for the opportunity to meet his next partner. All he needed now was to carry on with adeptness and a great deal of patience. It would be just a question of time. Hassan might just turn out to be a suitable instrument to the execution of his mission. An idea was looming at the back of Gamal's mind: "I could be his wrestling coach. I can suggest we practice together. I'll show him how good I am. Once I talk him into this, we'll be able to take the coaching a little bit further."

Wednesday, as Hassan entered the gym, Gamal made the proposition and heard Hassan reply with a question:

"Why do you want to be my wrestling coach? I'm only a practicing beginner with no intention of going pro."

"I've been eying you lately and I think that, for a beginner, you fight very well. I'm proficient in *vale-tudo* (anything goes) fighting, and I'm telling you that you could well be a coach yourself if you wanted. You probably don't need the job to earn your livelihood. Not my case. This is what I do and I have to make a living."

Hassan put his hands on his waist, hanged down his head for a moment and then raised it to stare into Gamal's eyes.

"Well, let me sleep on it. I like vale-tudo. I was never big on wrestling."

The terrorist smiled and crossed his arms.

"Listen, my friend, whoever is acquainted with more than one fighting style will never bite the dust. I mean, the odds will be overwhelmingly in his favor."

"Yeah, you're probably right. As I said, I'll sleep on it. Well, goodbye for now!" he said suddenly, turning away and heading over to the other side of the gym."

"This is one unsociable weirdo," he said in a murmur as he watched Hassan walk into the men's locker room.

Ibrahim Hassan had acquired the habit of, at least once a week, at night, driving his motorcycle down to the banks of Lake Paranoa. He would always end up at that same spot where he had spent a sleepless night when he left his house on the morning he read about the tragedy in the papers. It was quiet out there and he had staked himself out a piece of that ground. As in the first time around, he lay on his back at the foot of the hill, gazing up at the sky, letting his thoughts run free and trying to bring back memories of a recent past. As he thought about his misfortunes, his hatred of the assassin of his family increased. He had transferred all that anger on to the American ambassador. "That bastard needs to die, so I can go find my peace next to Raissa in Paradise."

One day, his team was given the afternoon off after a trip up North with the president, and Hassan spent it at the gym. At dusk he left the academy, gave Gamal a weary wave as he exited, and headed off to his "refuge" by the lake.

It did not take long for Hassan to notice that his bike was being tailed by a vehicle. He slowed down to make sure, and the car behind him followed suit. When he pulled on to the gravel road towards Paranoa, his pursuer braked off to the side of the road, made a U-turn and drove off, leaving behind a cloud of dust.

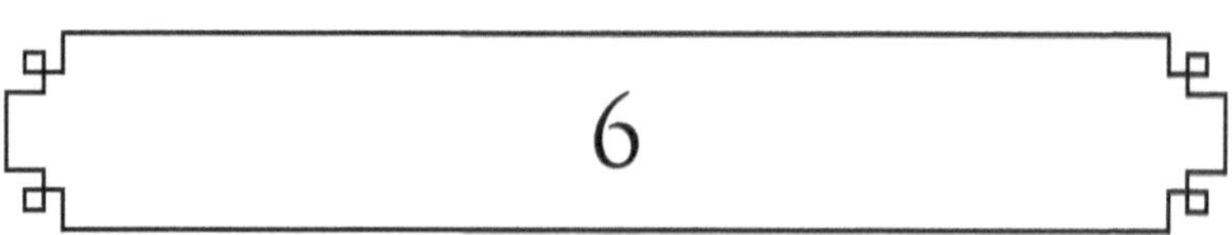

6

Deivid is a name open to more than one interpretation by those who are knowledgeable of both English and Portuguese with equal or nearly equal fluency. When pronounced according to Portuguese phonetics, it sounds like a foreign name to Brazilians. When spelled by anyone familiar with the branch of linguistics that deals with the sounds of speech, it is immediately assumed that this choice of orthography only reflects the parents' wish to have their child named David. Well, had they spelled it "David," people would say "Dahveed." There are many other similar cases in Brazil of parents who want their children to be named after personages of distinction from the English-speaking world. Therefore "Deivid" should be pronounced "David."

Anyway, Deivid de Souza was born in Taguatinga, a satellite town in the outskirts of Brasilia. Born into poverty he went to public schools, and in Brazil public schools are not well cared for; on the contrary, they are underfunded and indeed dangerous. Deivid pulled through. He graduated, joined the Army, and worked his way up to the noncommissioned rank of sergeant.

When Ibrahim Hassan was dragged into the president's staff by Lt. Col. Blake, he could not figure out how a fellow like Deivid ended up in the Presidential Palace three weeks later. The colonel barely knew him. Very few noticed the slimy manner which he managed to get included in the small work force that helped the Blake family unload the moving van. Oozing charm from every pore, he offered his volunteer services to bear a hand; and that was how he began to fawn on the boss, seeking his favor and attention by flattery and obsequious behavior. Deivid was shrewd, astute, crafty, and consumed by a baleful envy of Hassan. "I wonder what Blake sees in that cantankerous Arab who does nothing but suck up to his little boy."

Deivid's resentment reached its climax when Blake chose Hassan as one of his personal aides and sent him to work in the palace's garage, where vehicles of all sorts were repaired, serviced, or parked.

Sergeant Deivid's ambition ran much higher. He buckled down earnestly to get a post in the ultra-select team of secret service agents in charge of the president's protection. They had to be appointed by people who held a place high in the president's confidence. Openings were available only by demise, retirement or dishonorable discharge. The latter possibility was seldom the case, but it was not unheard-of. Deivid soon realized that for him to have a break it would be necessary to get rid of his colleague; the very same one who had introduced him to

Blake a few months ago to bear a hand with the moving van: Ibrahim Hassan.

"From today forward that Arab bastard won't have it so easy. I'll fix his wagon. I'll pry into every nook and corner of his life. I'll find a way to get him booted out of that coterie of privileged insiders."

Using all his devious cunning, Deivid started out by buttering up the security agents with plenty of flattery and cajolery to achieve his ends. He took extra care of their cars during his breaks and even swapped damaged parts for good ones that he had removed from the official vehicles. By and by he managed to make friends with everyone. Hassan was the only one Deivid slighted. "When it's his turn to get sacked big time, I'll suggest my own name to my future fellow agents. They will be the ones that will talk the colonel into hiring me on."

He began to follow Hassan around after gym hours. His scheme proceeded like clockwork and it seemed to be going off very smoothly. Deivid kept on Hassan's tail almost every day. He could now do it from a carefully chosen distance, because he had already sussed out all the Arab's routes. They never changed.

"This guy has no life. From the Palace he heads straight for home, and then it's the gym or the colonel's home to sit with that spoiled brat or the mosque or that lakeside slope way off the beaten track. He doesn't hang out with women. Agent Carlos says he must be a mi…so… misogynist. Yeah! That's it, that's the word: misogynist! What the hell is a misogynist? I'll have to swing by a bookstore and buy me a frigging dictionary one of these days." With these thoughts on his mind he turned left near the mosque and pulled on to the freeway, heading home.

But this time it was Hassan's turn to follow him. He was surprised to see the car be driven into the noncommissioned officers' housing area. From afar, cursing out the lack of a good pair of binoculars, he could see the car pull up on one of the driveways, but it was impossible to recognize who got out of it and went into the house. "I know where you live. I'll find out who you are," he muttered with a tone of contentment.

He eased down the accelerator of his motorcycle and drove away slowly.

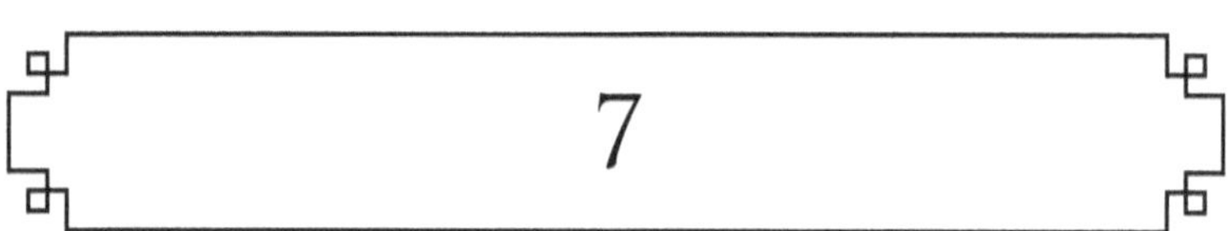

7

Meanwhile, in Lisbon, Tiago, one of Eduardo Santana's brothers, put a long-distance call through to his other brother Mauricio, the detective.

"Eduardo was murdered. Mayhem here, brother, big time. Unbearable pain." He briefly let Mauricio in on what had happened. "City police are investigating. Doing the best they can, I guess. I had to tell you immediately. Think you can help?"

Under the impact of the terrible news, Mauricio managed to say: "I'll be up there first thing tomorrow." However, leaving from Luanda, with all the delays, his plane landed in Lisbon only late at night.

In the morning, all bundled up against the bitter cold, Mauricio headed straight to the precinct. He was 5 ft. 11 in, had a fair complexion, gently curly brown hair, and green eyes. He looked in on the district chief of police, Jose Maria Gonçalves, in charge of the case.

"I started off at the inn where the body was found," said the chief, after the usual greetings and words of condolences. "I brought in the lodgers for questioning. Already heard all of them. There seems to be no doubt that the killer is an Arab who calls himself Mohammed Salik. He was your brother's bunkmate. Vanished without a trace."

Mauricio was sitting in a chair across from the chief's desk.

"Now it comes to mind," he said. "Last Sunday, during lunch with my parents and brothers up in Braga, Eduardo mentioned this Arab. Said he was a gentleman, a real nice guy. Ironic as it may sound, Eduardo had even invited him to come to lunch with us. This Mohammed told him he couldn't make it, because he needed to seek out a school for his cookery lessons. Yeah! That was it. The Arab wanted to be a cook and make a living in Brazil."

The chief was silent and thoughtful for a moment.

"I reckon he ran off to Brazil then…"

"I concur."

Jose Maria searched the computer for the airlines flying out to Brazil since Wednesday. According to the coroner, the crime had been committed between Tuesday at 8 p.m. and Wednesday at 4 a.m. The Arab had probably made his escape around four o'clock in the morning. The chief pulled up the data on the computer and found out that TAP and Continental Airlines had daily flights to Brazil, departing at 6 a.m. TAP flew nonstop to Sao Paulo, and Continental made a stopover in Newark, NJ.

"He must've flown TAP to avoid American paranoia against Arabs," said Mauricio, now standing next to Jose Maria as he searched the Internet.

"Most likely. Let's check whether his name appears on any of the passenger lists to Brazil on Wednesday, Thursday, or this morning," the chief rattled off as he reached for the phone and dialed a number.

There's no Mohammed Salik listed anywhere. The only Arabic name is Gamal Abdul. He took off on the 6:05 a.m. TAP flight on Wednesday.

"This is our man!" exclaimed Mauricio when he heard the chief repeat the information, jotting the name down on a piece of paper. "Abdul Gamal."

"Well, Brazil is huge. How do we go about finding him? Jose Maria sounded discouraged.

"Do we have a police sketch?"

"I've set up an appointment here with four volunteers for a composite sketch at noon today. They may have important details for a good facial composite."

"Four of them, heh! Even better." Mauricio glanced at his wristwatch. "What time is it? "We have a little less than half an hour to go. I think I'll tag along. Is it OK?"

"Sure, be my guest! You're Interpol, not to mention you're also that poor kid's brother."

They chatted over other subsequent steps to be taken in Portugal and Brazil, until three young men and one young woman were ushered in.

The identification by means of superimposed images made by a police expert summoned by Jose Maria was quick and bore a nearly identical resemblance to the murderer. After minor adjustments as to the description of the color of the eyes, complexion, hairstyle, particular marks etc., one of the boys cried out:

"That's our man! That's him all over, isn't it?" he looked around at his companions.

"That's him!" was the unison reply.

A young man, apparently the leader of the group, remarked in a solemn tone:

"You gentlemen are now in possession of a foolproof portrait of the assassin. All you have to do is send him off to prison and throw away the key."

Jose Maria pulled a long sigh.

"Son, I wish it were as easy as you imagine! All the bad guys in the world would be in jail."

"Will you still be needing us here, sir?" the girl asked.

"No, thank you ever so much for you precious help! You may go now. Please, leave your names and addresses with the officer at the reception desk."

The two policemen didn't see them leave, for they had their eyes fixed on the facial composite of Mohammed Gamal Abdul Salik. After running off a number of copies, they both decided to pay a visit to Mauricio's boss at the Interpol office.

Together with Lisbon police investigator Jose Maria Gonçalves and his own Interpol chief Joaquim Andrade, detective Mauricio Santana looked over a large number of photographs and drawings of most wanted terrorists and compared them with that of Mohammed Salik or Gamal Abdul.

"Nothing," he said after a while.

"If he really is a terrorist, nobody knows anything about him. His face doesn't match any of these.

"Maybe he belongs to some undetected cell," Joaquim Andrade suggested.

"Speaking from our experience, everything leads to the sound assumption that he is a terrorist," Jose Maria interjected. "But what if we are wrong?"

"He's got to be a terrorist," Mauricio argued. "This is not about the way he looks, but what my brother told me about him. An idle vagrant with money in his pocket, trying to learn a new trade to get a job in another country. It doesn't make much sense, does it?"

Joaquim Andrade concurred:

"He plum shows up out of the blue, seeking out a profession at this point and time in life, when money is no problem for him. Then he commits a barbaric murder, does not steal anything from the victim, and disappears. This scenario clearly points to a terrorist."

"I wonder what Eduardo may have discovered about this Arab for him to decide to waste him," Mauricio pondered with eyes fixed on the spoken portrait.

"I keep asking myself that very same question," said Jose Maria.

Joaquim interjected: "Maybe this Mohammed… This name's got to be fake… Maybe he let out more than he intended… Maybe he was doing something self-implicating and your brother caught him in the act."

"How unfortunate! My brother was only nineteen. He was just a boy."

They chatted it over, made conjectures, and looked for clues, but always returned to the starting point.

Picking up one of the pictures from the stack next to him, Chief Joaquim Andrade addressed Mauricio:

"Pack it up! You're going to Brazil. I'll call ahead to the Interpol branch in Sao Paulo and ask for their help. But it'll be up to you to smoke out this scoundrel," he stuck his finger in Gama's face. "Cuff him up and put him behind bars. Then you just let me know. I'll personally yank the motive for this vile murder out of him."

"Are you acquainted with the head honcho of Interpol in Sao Paulo?" asked Jose Maria.

"Commissioner Cerveira? No, not personally. We talk on the phone every now and then. He is cooperative, always willing to help. That's Brazil for you. They are our natural kinfolk so to speak. I'm sure Cerveira will give Mauricio all the support he needs."

Mauricio gathered up a few copies of Gamal's portrait and put them in his briefcase.

"May I shove off day after tomorrow?"

"You'd better."

The meeting was over. Joaquim stood up. José Maria put out his hand and thanked him. "Thanks for your big help."

They all bade farewell to each other.

"I'll call you from Brazil."

"Sure. Let's communicate by e-mail, too."

"As you wish, sir."

"Good luck, boy!"

Maurício and Jose Maria left the office. Joaquim Andrade sat down behind his desk, reached for his phone and put a long-distance call through to Brazil.

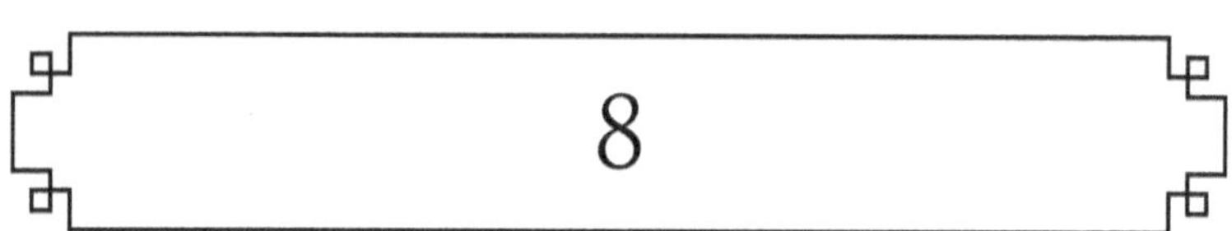

8

The first preparatory meeting for the ceremony of the signing of the agreement addressing the gradual replacement of oil with alternative sources of energy, now dubbed The Diversified Fuel Event, was held on the 1st of August. Brazilian government officials had drafted the outlines of the agenda on which the announcement of this date was recorded. A high-level attendance by foreign dignitaries was expected along with their respective secret service escorts. Heads of government and state, ministers, advisors, and even military top brass had been confirmed.

Given the positions coveted by bodyguards, usually close to the target they are supposed to protect in the daily grind of dealing with all sorts of difficult figures in high posts, the order and harmony of their eventual association with other secret services are especially susceptible to a bonfire of vanities, arrogance, and haughtiness. Therefore, their consortium is always an arduous task to handle when organizing strict schedules and selecting venues. Even agents from the same country sometimes behave like incidental competitors when such susceptibilities clash thus jeopardizing an effective interaction. Knowing this, Defense Minister Dario Fortes assisted by the Commandant of the Navy, Admiral Juliano Soares, took the floor and spoke out without preamble:

"The Americans are prone to be a hindrance under the pretext of shoring up the safety of their own president. They always do that. They may even come to the point of proposing that we should desist with our own security measures and let them take over," his mouth curved into a scornful smile. "Well, not on my watch. As defense minister I deem this sort of claim uncalled-for. Admiral Soares here and myself have concocted stringent safety measures to be stepped up around and on board the aircraft carrier Rio de Janeiro with the cooperation of the Commandant of the Army, General André Sousa, and also of the Commandant of the Air Force here with us today," pointing to Brigadier Silas. "We can provide better security for our distinguished guests in a more timely, cost-efficient, and effective manner than could be done by anybody else on our own turf. When we meet again, there'll be representatives from all the countries involved, and I expect your undivided attention and support. I will start out by outlining our strategy, and then I'll cut short any notion of outside interference. We are within our unquestionable right to dictate security policy in our homeland. I daresay that foreign meddling is out of the question." He was given a standing ovation.

The home secretary, Abelardo Mendes, meeting coordinator, expressed his discreet approval of Fortes's speech by clapping his hands in a gesture marked by self-restraint and reticence. He respected his colleague, knowing him for a serious, determined, responsible politician at the head of a rather critical ministry, the remit of which included very specific features. The commandants of the armed services under Fortes in the chain of command had had the nub of leadership in their veins ever since they joined the service. They were true patriots, highly organized and extremely professional. Disdainful of politicians, the military commanders knew they had taken their oaths to serve their country, namely the State, the supreme public power within a sovereign political entity, and not merely a fleeting administration, whereas Mendes, seen as a feeble figure, was kept in office only because he had been a long-time party activist and a close friend of the president's; in short, a grafter.

Nevertheless, it was up to the commanders of the Armed Forces to explain how they intended to enhance security during the event at hand. In the end, all actions and procedures were rehashed regarding the upcoming meeting with the foreign representatives. It was also decided that from that date forward the members of the staff who would actually play an important role in the scheme would gradually and confidentially be notified. Each sector was to initiate arrangements for the event as to the necessary logistics and communications so that every contingency would be satisfactorily covered on the 15th of October, the D-Day for the conclusion of the agreements.

Immediately after the meeting, Colonel William Blake assembled his henchmen in the briefing room:

"As soon as I'm done talking here, I want you to scramble to your usual preliminary chores on the double to avoid last-minute rush and delays when D-Day dawns on us. Until further instructions this matter is classified. Any questions so far?"

The audience remained silent.

"OK, listen up! There will be a great event this coming October 15th aboard our aircraft carrier lying at anchor in Guanabara Bay." He paused. "In Rio, of course." The men smiled. "The presidents of Brazil, the United States, Mexico, Venezuela will attend…" He went on to explain the general idea and some of the particulars, stressing the nature and advantages of the agreement, etc.

The briefing was adjourned and the men dismissed.

"Hassan, you come with me," said Blake, after the other agents were out of earshot.

They went into the colonel's office. The door was locked behind them. Blake motioned Hassan to a seat.

"I'm going to pick out the best men for this job on October 15th regarding the protection of our president. Since the American president will be there, probably standing next to our president, we will have to be extra careful, because we know those Gringos are very exacting and demanding, not to say downright picky. You're hereby assigned to be our key liaison element with the U.S. secret agents during the ceremony. That puts you on the side closest to President Brian. I'll be right next to you on your right and behind our president. Anything happen, I'll be counting on you. Do you read me?"

"Loud and clear, sir! I'm honored with your trust."

"Practice your English. Thank you. That will be all for now. Dismissed!"

Hassan got up, stood at attention, did an about-face, and left the room.

He went back to his desk and tried to put a little order in his confused mind.

"What am I going to do now? Will I manage to be alive until October 15th? By then the ambassador and I are supposed to be goners."

Disillusioned with life and eager to go find his Raissa in paradise, Ibrahim Hassan started behaving like a robot: he did not exercise his human ability to reason. He practiced his fighting skills with no enthusiasm and consistently bit the canvas. The reckless driving of his motorcycle constantly put him in harm's way. His only source of enjoyment was playing with Guto, when his mind wandered and his thoughts turned to the sweet memories of Raissa and the orphanage children. Hassan sometimes felt a brief puff of contentment as he lay down at night on the shores of Paranoa Lake, flirting with the stars. He associated those moments by the still waters and under the sky with his soon-to-happen cohabitation with his bride in heaven. According to the Koran — and Hassan read from the sacred text of Islam every single day — the paradise he was to share with Raissa in the near future was described as a place with comfortable mansions, beautiful gardens, fruits, wealth, and servants.

At the close of working hours, Hassan headed straight for the gym. He needed to cool off his head because an important decision had to be made: should he carry out his plan before or after that fateful October 15th? The ongoing month was August, so he had time to think the whole thing out. After several days, although struggling with reluctance, he argued himself into practicing his fighting skills with Gamal Abdul.

At least twice a week, they worked out in the gym. Occasionally, at dusk, they would meet up at the mosque for prayers. Always open to members and students, the Academy Gym was very well-attended, especially late in the day and in the evening until ten o'clock; a wholesome milieu that was a place of contentment and casual conversation and a source of agreeable leisure for those who fought professionally or practiced self-defense as a hobby. It was the perfect spot to start up a conversation and make new friends, and to get to know people better.

After two months, however distrustful, Hassan eased off on his language monosyllabic responses and managed to actually strike up short conversations with Gamal.

When he had to travel for a couple of days or longer, he gave the excuse of having to accompany his boss, a wealthy business executive who took frequent trips to Sao Paulo, Rio de Janeiro, Belo Horizonte, and some cities located in the countryside of Sao Paulo State, like Americana and Sao Jose dos Campos.

"What's your job?" asked Gamal.

"I'm a sort-of bodyguard, secretary, and errand boy all rolled into one."

"You always travel by plane?"

"Nah! Sometimes we drive. It's up to my boss, Mr. Lario."

Gamal was wary of this story, but he was also very patient and usually proceeded in an observant, prescribed pattern of behavior. There was no doubt in his mind that the truth would soon rise to the surface.

During his respites from work, usually in the evening, Hassan sometimes went by the colonel's residence to spend time with Guto. He could not quite make his reasons plain nor did he realize that Guto filled up the deepest gap in his need to bring back the orphanage children into his life, a time when he had Raissa; and Guto was the only living link with the object of his mourning.

In those short visits, both the colonel and Dona Leticia treated him with great consideration and always expressed their thankfulness. They often invited him to dinner, but Hassan seldom accepted; and when he did, it turned out to be one of those rather peculiar, embarrassing, awkward, typically "Hassanic" situations: Hassan ate very little, barely spoke, and seemed to be ill at ease. So the couple preferred to leave him alone with the boy, and they had their dinner only after he had left.

One afternoon, Hassan came to the gym in a bad mood. He had read in the newspaper that the American ambassador was stateside on vacation. This news spelled another delay in his project.

When Gamal waved him over, Hassan refused to go to practice.

"What are you doing here then?"

"Snooping around; prowling, actually. Every time I leave the gym, some clown tries to tail me around in a car. Today I'm determined to clear up this racket."

"Most of the time, you go straight to the mosque. Does he still follow you then?"

"He does. There's a car on my tail. When I get to the temple, he puts about and disappears."

"Well, it's not me. Do you have any idea as to who he might be?"

"No! I know it isn't you. Last night, it was my turn to tail him without his knowing it. Since the first time I drove out to the refuge, he..." he cut himself short, his instincts screaming at him to hold his tongue. He had let on too much.

"Refuge! Did you say refuge?"

"Forget it. I'm pushing off!"

Hassan turned his back and walked away. He went to the mosque for his prayers.

The next day Gamal Abdul was teaching the first moves of wrestling to a beginner when he saw Hassan walk in and go straight into the men's locker room. He kept an eye out for Hassan lest that screwed-up, elusive figure would vanish all of a sudden. Gamal could hardly wait to show him the used bike he had bought from one of his students. When Hassan emerged from the locker room he was still fully dressed. Gamal asked his disciple to take five. He approached Hassan.

"Aren't you practicing today?"

"Still debating. I got a few problems to solve. I think I'm going to the mosque to pray for guidance. After that, well, I'll just go for a ride."

"Can I help?"

"No. Nobody can."

"I'd like to show you my bike."

"You bought a motorcycle?"

"I did. Come on! I want to know what you think."

Together they walked to the parking lot. Hassan wore a jacket and tie; Gamal was in his instructor's sweat suit.

"Here she is!" Gamal pointed to a blue motorcycle parked alongside of Hassan's.

"Just like mine. A fine piece of machine."

"There's a slight difference," said Gamal. "Yours is a brand new one. This one is a five-year old model. I spent my life's savings on this baby."

Hassan didn't answer. He just climbed on his own bike and drove off. Gamal watched him go, muttering: "Now I can follow you. I need to find out who you really are. I need to learn about the problems that have been tormenting you, oh ye abstruse Hassan!"

In the mosque, Hassan said his prayers. There was still light out, so he drove down to the Army housing compound. He was looking for the house of the man who had followed him out to the lake on the other night.

As he approached the small square he slowed down and parked down the street behind a tree where he hid his bike. Bitterly regretting once again the lack of binoculars, he crossed over to the other sidewalk where he had seen his follower park. Since the residential units were like townhouses, it was hard to tell the door by which he had entered. Suddenly Hassan saw the headlights of a car coming towards him. Startled, he halted, turned on his heels, and bolted back to the tree. He saw the car park in front one of the houses, and a woman with a number of children got out of it. He thought it best to call it a day and went home. He did not even notice Deivid's car speed by on the freeway. Deivid did not see him either.

9

In the taxi to Portela airport, his heart clouded with rage for his brother's killer, Mauricio remembered one of Sinead O'Connors's lyrics, "And, if you make your bed in hell, I will be there…" for such was his determination to find that terrorist. His design was to arrest him or maybe even kill the bastard if it came to that; somehow he would fulfill his duty to avenge Eduardo's death.

He flew TAP to Sao Paulo.

During the flight he read and reread his notes. That brief record he had written down to aid his memory would help him in his hunt. For a long time he looked out the window as the plane soared above a dense blanket of white clouds. He plunged into memories of Eduardo, the baby brother who looked up to him and wanted to follow in his footsteps. "Your niggling will do no good to nobody", the kid had said. "I'm gonna be a cop just like you. End of story."

In fact the two brothers who occupied the lower and upper ends of a string of five boys were very much alike and had a great deal in common. Eduardo was 19 years old at his demise and Mauricio was 32 years of age. Mauricio put his kid brother through college, since their father, meagerly retired from the Postal Service, could not afford it. "Suddenly, some unknown son of a bitch pops out of nowhere and puts an end to my brother's existence," he thought in a jolt of anger. "Well, let me paraphrase O'Connor: you can hide your ass in hell, and I'll smoke it out…"

"Would you like steak or fish?" the flight attendant was taking down the lunch orders.

"Oh, forgive me, I am in such an abstracted mood today," he said. "I'll have the fish, please."

Mauricio turned his eyes back to the clouds. His trip down memory lane was replaced by a pleasanter thought: he was finally going to see Brazil, a travel option that — when he had the time — was usually discarded in favor of more sophisticated destinations in Europe, such as France, Italy, England, and the like.

The flight was smooth and relaxing. By nightfall the huge plane landed at the airport of Guarulhos, taxied down the runway and parked at the assigned gate where a jetbridge was mated to the fuselage. As usual the disembarkation of passengers was bureaucratically marked by unremitting sameness.

Mauricio was glad to be welcomed by a Brazilian Interpol colleague at the airport arrival lounge.

"My name is Acioly, Agent Francisco Acioly. We're fellow members of our profession. I'm pleased to meet you!"

The agent put out his hand. "Have a nice trip?"

"Pleasure's all mine." They shook hands. "Trip was just fine, thank you."

"I'll drive you to your hotel, Hotel Paissandu. It's not far from our office."

"I am obliged to you for your gracious hospitality."

On the way over, they exchanged notes on the case. At the hotel lounge, Mauricio asked:

"What time do we meet tomorrow?"

"At 9:30 a van will come by to pick you up, if that's OK with you."

"That'll be just fine by me. Again, I'm most thankful to you. See you tomorrow!"

"Have a nice evening!"

Mauricio got settled in his room, took a long, hot shower, and had dinner at the hotel's restaurant. He went to bed early, watched the nine o'clock news, and, exhausted as he was, fell asleep.

After saying good night to the Portuguese detective, Acioly drove back to the Interpol office.

"Mission accomplished, Boss! I dropped the man off at the hotel. Well mannered, congenial... Quite handsome I'd say."

"I can see you are impressed."

"Indeed I am. We chatted about the case. His heart is set on finding the man who killed his brother."

"I didn't know the victim was his brother," interjected Agent Fontana, who was slouched in an armchair across from Commissioner Cerqueira's desk.

"Yeah, he told me his kid brother shared a room in a hostel with the killer. His name is Mauricio, and he is convinced this Arab is a terrorist."

"I'll appoint one of you guys to help him in this investigation," said Cerqueira lighting a cigarette.

"That'll be a hell of a snag," said Acioly. "The whole staff is engaged in the inquest concerning the gang headed by that Colombian from the Andrulla cartel."

"Except yourself!" said Cerqueira.

"Me? I'll be off to Santos tomorrow morning to join the Feds in the inspection of those containers suspected of carrying smuggled cocaine into the country? Bet you forgot all about that."

Cerqueira dragged on his cigarette and let out a bluish, gray puff from his lips and nostrils, polluting the air.

"OK, I've got it!" he exclaimed.

"Who?" asked Acioly.

"Raquel. Raquel will be his partner."

"Don't you think this job is a little too much over the top for Raquel, I mean, she's a woman and… I mean, what if we're really dealing with terrorists here?"

"I don't think so! Raquel is pretty tough, a hard bone to pick. Nobody pushes her around. Once I had to hold her back because she wanted to hit a prisoner. The poor dumb bastard suggested that, being just a plain bimbo, she couldn't possibly cut it as a cop."

"Apart from the macho bit you're right, sir. She radiates a personal magnetism and a strong personality," said Acioly.

"And she isn't half bad-looking, either," added Fontana.

Cerqueira didn't want to go there. He smashed out his cigarette in the full ashtray.

"Fontana, you tell Raquel to saddle up and be ready," he said. "She will be Portuguese Detective Mauricio Santana's partner. She'll travel with him if it comes to that,"

He cleared his throat before going on.

"Acioly, I want all of you in the briefing room at 11 a.m. tomorrow. Do not go off to Santos before passing the word to everyone. I'll introduce Mauricio to the staff and introduce Raquel to Mauricio."

Cerqueira stood up, looked at his watch, reached for his jacket on the back of his chair, and was about to stroll out the door when Aciocy said: "I've got an idea. Why don't you assign Marcos instead of Raquel?"

"Are you crazy? That xenophobe is bound to start up a diplomatic incident."

"The boss is right," said Fontana. "That guy is nuts. No normal human being can be so unduly fearful and contemptuous of that which is foreign, especially of strangers from foreign countries. He is so wacko that he even gratuitously dislikes fellow Brazilians who hail from outside of São Paulo. Talk about neurotics!"

Cerqueira put on his jacket and decided to call it a day. "That's all folks! See you all tomorrow."

It was a clear morning out, with wisps of clouds visible here and there in the pale blue sky. The meeting started promptly at eleven o'clock. That was how the overly punctual Cerqueira liked. He did not abide tardiness. The eye-catching emblem of Interpol on red copper shimmered in the sunlight coming through the cracks of the moldy blinds. It is a representation of the globe to indicate INTERPOL's worldwide activities. The olive branches either side of the globe symbolize peace. The scales below the olive branches stand for justice. A vertical sword behind the globe represents police action, and the name " 'INTERPOL" is displayed below the globe in the center of the olive branches.

Cerqueira sat at the head of the table next to Detective Mauricio Santana. He made the introductions, leaving Agent Raquel Lopes for last and announcing that she was now the Portuguese colleague's partner.

"I want to talk to the two of you in my office right after this meeting," the commissioner said.

The meeting went on, and during just over an hour they discussed issues pertaining to investigations in progress. Individual Instructions were given on the sequence of activities to be performed by all agents and their reports had to be turned in upon completion.

"Before closing, I recommend that as soon as you're done writing your reports just lay them on my desk. Don't wait until the last minute of Friday to do it. I want to avoid the paper pile-ups that force me to work over the weekend on your reports. It's rather exhausting."

When the meeting was adjourned Raquel and Mauricio joined the commissioner in his office.

"I give you both carte blanche to act independently in the conduction of this investigation to find the man who killed that boy. Talk it out, exchange ideas, and decide on the most acceptable course of action. You are both capable and intelligent agents. I know this from reading your resume," he pointed to Raquel, "and talking to the Lisbon chief of police on the phone." He smiled at Mauricio. I've destined a special budget to cover travel expenses, including lodging and meals." He addressed Raquel: "It's already been deposited in your account." He turned to the Portuguese detective: "You can set about solving this crime directly!"

Cerqueira shook hands with them and stood by as they left the room.

Somewhat astounded by that sudden display of unemotional straightforwardness, Mauricio followed Raquel over to her desk.

"Is your boss always like this?"

She smiled. "Invariably. He wants things done with no waste of time."

"You know something, Miss Lopes? I like him."

"OK, no more of this Miss and Mister business. From now on I'll be Raquel and you, Mauricio. Sound good to you?"

"Fair enough. Thanks."

After reviewing all the facts germane to the crime, Raquel evinced her commiseration for the loss of Mauricio's brother. She suggested that they go out to lunch. It was past two o'clock.

During lunch, while they chatted and waited for their orders, Mauricio appraised the young woman, and he could not help musing: "By golly, she's hot! Seems to be so firm, so determined, so unwavering. I wonder if she's married."

His thoughts were broken up by Raquel's voice.

"Are you alright?"

"Huh? Who? Me? Sure. I'm fine, thank you. Why?

"You seemed so far away. Thinking of Portugal?

"Oh, no, not really! I'm just amazed at how things are happening so quickly."

"Indeed they are! Now we set out on a different kind of hunt for us Brazilians: the target is a possible terrorist. We're used to tracking down and arresting drug dealers and traffickers; but when it comes to terrorists, this is all new to me. I mean, the real thing, those who engage in acts of extreme violence against people or property or even nations with the intention of intimidating or coercing societies or governments, often for ideological or political reasons. There was the AMIA bombing in Argentina, of course; an attack on the Jewish Community Center building in Buenos Aires on July 18, 1994, that killed 85 people and injured 300. It was Argentina's deadliest bombing. Well, in 2006, during a police raid on drug trafficking at Iguazu Falls two Lebanese, father and son, were arrested for operating a drug cache. They were found to be members of Hezbollah, the Iranian-backed Lebanese terrorist organization, and wanted in the United States. The Argentine government announced that both men were tied to the bombing. Such allegations are controversial, especially within the region. Critics contend that no solid evidence has been offered for al Qaeda involvement, claiming that this is a case of regional demographic profiling. Connections with the Lebanese Shiite militia Hezbollah, however, are better substantiated. This was all over the media and it just about covers everything I know about chasing terrorists."

"When we get back to the office, let's ask Lisbon for copies of the tapes from the airport security cameras that match the days we assume the killer boarded his flight," Mauricio suggested.

"Good idea! We'll request the same thing from Guarulhos."

After lunch they returned to the office and e-mailed their respective law enforcement branches. They both had direct access to the administration of all airports in the free world. They got down to comparing the photographs of terrorists wanted by the police with the facial composite of Gamal Abdul.

They called it a day in the early evening and parted with a handshake.

When Mauricio came to Raquel's desk in the morning it was tem minutes past nine.

"I didn't expect this much traffic at this hour," he said looking at his watch.

"I'm usually on time, but I'm not as punctual as commissioner Cerqueira. Ten minutes early or late don't faze me any," Raquel said looking at him with an enchanting smile as he pulled up a chair and sat in front of her desk.

"How are you this morning, Miss Lopes?"

"You mean Raquel, right? Not Miss Lopes. Well, I'm fine, thank you. You Portuguese are very formal and polite and so very observant of accepted social usage. Try to 'Brazilianize' yourself a bit… kind of just for a few days. It'll make our lives easier and you will fit right in with the tropical scene."

"It's a deal. I promise!" Mauricio said, blushing a little."

Spreading a map of Brazil on her desk, Raquel expressed her views on the case at hand.

"I was thinking… If the murderer is still here in Sao Paulo, there is a chance, however far-fetched, of getting the dope on his whereabouts. Today I'll hand over copies of the police sketch to my informant in the underworld. I bet you do the same thing in Portugal, and so does every decent cop all over the world," she said smiling. "Later on this evening, we will take a stroll around the dark side of town where all kinds of weirdoes are engaged in or organized for the purpose of crime and vice. I'll take these three copies to this ex-convict I know. He owes me a few favors. He'll ask around if anyone saw this Gamal."

"Well, so far it seems our field-search methods are very similar," said Mauricio.

"We're bound to have some sort of feedback only very late at night. Between now and then, I propose that we try to dig up all there is to know or to infer concerning the presence of terrorists in Brazil. We ought to look into this together."

"Terrorists are shifty, slippery, and inscrutable. Very seldom do we have a break that will allow us to establish the identity of one of them."

"I hear you. We have documents sent by the Americans on the presence of terrorists here." She put her finger on the map. "This area, called the Triple Frontier, including Iguaçu Falls and the patch of land that separates Brazil from Paraguay and Argentina, is a hiding place for terrorists, according to the CIA."

Mauricio did not interrupt her. He just sat there with his eyes glued on the map.

"The Triple Frontier is this tri-border area right here along the junction of Paraguay, Argentina, and Brazil," she went on. "That is one lawless area of illicit activities that generate billions of dollars annually in money laundering, arms and drug trafficking, counterfeiting, document falsification, and piracy. We will probably be heading down there after we hear from my informant, in case the killer is not hiding here in Sao Paulo."

"I read something about this a few years ago. If memory serves me right the Americans were attempting to send troops to that region."

"Well, yes, but Brazil would never agree to anything like that. Controversy raged in Paraguay, though. The U.S. military conducted secretive operations down there. Five hundred U.S. troops arrived in the country with planes, weapons and ammunition. Eyewitness reports prove that an airbase exists in Mariscal Estigarribia, Paraguay, which is 125 miles from the border with Bolivia and may be used by the U.S. military at any moment. Officials in Paraguay claim the military operations are routine humanitarian efforts and deny that any plans are underway for a U.S. base. Yet left wing groups in the area are furious. White House officials are using rhetoric about terrorist threats in the triborder region in order to build their case for military operations, in many ways reminiscent to the buildup to the invasion of Iraq. It is a fact that on May 26, 2005, the Paraguayan Senate granted the U.S. troops total immunity from national and International Criminal Court jurisdiction until December 2006. The legislation is automatically extendable at any time. But the reaction is so intense that the U.S. is bound to back down. Let's find out what the scenario is nowadays."

"Well, outside of São Paulo, we at least have a clue as to where to begin, don't you think?" said Mauricio. He was content to gain the awareness of something he had not known for sure up to this moment: his partner's police skills were far greater than her astonishing looks.

10

The day came for the meeting of The Diversified Fuel Event organizers with the participation of foreign representatives. Things turned out just as expected. The Americans, overly concerned about the safety of their president, proposed a major operation which was immediately warded off by Defense Minister Dario Fortes. After powwowing for a long time, they finally came to an agreement acceptable to Dario: the American president's secret service agents would proceed in the same manner and have the same freedom of action as the other presidential bodyguards on the flight deck of the carrier around their respective chiefs. They would all basically follow the same procedure. Indeed, the talks took a sharp turn for the minister's standpoint when it became known about the presence of five thousand men scattered across the shorelines, at airports, and on the box girder bridge that runs across the bay and connects the cities of Rio de Janeiro and Niteroi. Also, undercover agents would blend into the guests and reporters unnoticed; explosive-sniffing dogs would be sitting at the foot of the well-guarded gangway plank; a screen of ten men-of-war would be lying at anchor all around the carrier; ten military helicopters would be hovering over throughout the ceremony; and the bulk of the armed forces would be in top readiness condition with four jet fighters in the air and another four ready to take off in five minutes to intercept any possible threat. Security was extremely tight. Moreover, for the duration of the event, all commercial and private flights were canceled 30 nautical miles all around. The airports would be shut down until one hour after the end of the ceremony. All radars would be cobbled together into a system capable of covering every patch of the sky.

"In closing," said the Brazilian defense minister, "let me add that two submerged submarines will stand by in key positions, with all sensors on active mode, feeling out for strange noises in the water; and sixty divers will take turns around and under the flattop." The Minister enjoyed flaunting his knowledge of naval jargon.

Still the American representative was not happy. He wanted to know whether the agents involved would be doubled-checked by all the secret services.

"Even as we speak," replied the minister. "Any more questions?"

The simultaneous interpreters were swift and precise in translating back and forth, from and into Portuguese, English, Spanish, and other, diverse languages. The Argentine representative was next.

"Will there be many other guests besides political authorities and their entourages?"

"Yes, by all means! Businessmen and entrepreneurs from the countries involved and of course the families of all participants and organizers. There will be detectors and x-rays, and everybody has agreed to cooperate in case someone needs to be frisked. After all, ladies and gentleman, we're talking a celebration here, not a visit to a penitentiary."

There were a few smiles and giggles.

The minister downed the rest of his water in a couple of quick gulps. His glass was immediately refilled by a yeoman.

"And, by the way, this last question brings us to the issue of invited guests. I wish to remind you all that it is paramount to contact us through your embassies in order to obtain a copy of the manual on the security procedures regarding guests and other contingencies. We can't do this informally, because the document is classified and all copies are numbered and will have to be accounted for. This little red tape is for our own good. Finally, let's not forget that each country can only bring a maximum of thirty guests. Thank you, ladies and gentlemen."

He was applauded by all present.

A few more administrative questions of less relevance were addressed to the diplomats in the minister's staff before the meeting was adjourned.

As he was leaving the room, the minister overheard someone say:

"Security measures are way too exaggerated for this event."

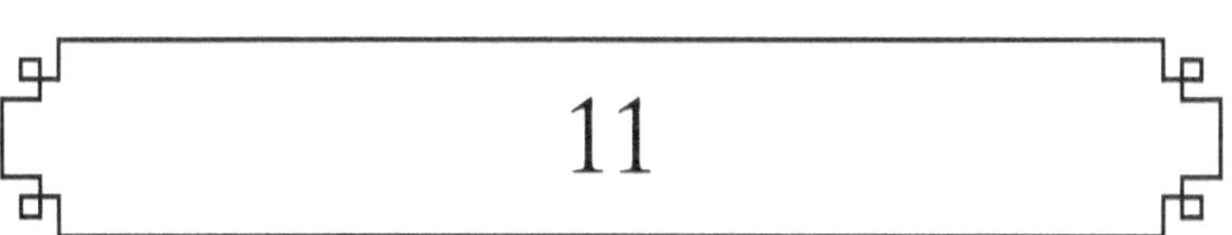

11

During a lunch break, while he installed a set of valves — pilfered from the storeroom where the spare parts for official vehicles were stowed — into the engine block of Homero's car, Deivid inserted a parenthetical remark, "I wonder if it would be hard to join the president's security detail..."

Grateful to have someone taking care of his private car with no costs, Homero phrased a tactful, political reply: "To be honest with you, I really don't know. When we're called up" — he carefully left out that they were appointed by high-ranking authorities — "we're tested for fighting skills, high proficiency in shooting firearms, and they put us through a lot of physical exams and psychological tests. Do you have any special fighting skills? Can you shoot straight? Do you work out regularly?"

Deivid was filled with a sudden wonder, edging towards disbelief. For him this piece of information was unanticipated and way out of the ordinary. He was caught unawares, because he had never known that Hassan had undergone such a battery of exams and tests.

"How strange," he said. "I didn't know Hassan was any good with hand weapons or adept at fighting."

"Who? The Arab? Are you kidding? Just for you to have an idea, a slight notion, mind you, of his prowess, let me tell you that he scored 98 out of 100 marksmanship points. It's a historic record in this man's Army. He's strong as a horse, if not stronger. I saw all the practical applicant tests to ascertain his qualifications. I'm telling you… He beat the examiner three times in a row… laid him out like a blanket. Deivid, you really don't know the Arab. He's a regular Rambo. I know it. I've seen him in the field during training. When it comes to the Arab, I'm telling you, one has to accept the fact we're dealing with an expert in guerrilla warfare, with a man who's the best, with guns, with knives, with his bare hands… like that character Rambo from the movies. Like Rambo Hassan's been trained to ignore pain, ignore weather, to live off the land, to eat things that would make a billy goat puke. Well, he's the best. And he practices, and works out at the gym every day."

Deivid was flabbergasted.

"Oh boy! I didn't know he was that good. But what about his psychological test?"

"Now that I wouldn't know. Nobody would. It's classified. But I know he was cleared pronto with no need for a retake or anything," Homero said using their current lingo.

After replacing the last valve, Deivid started the engine, revved it up, and checked a few gauges.

"And we're good to go. This is as good as it gets. Brand new! It won't go dead on you any time soon. By the way, do you think I'll have a chance to join the team if I learn how to shoot and fight?"

Again, Homero was uneasy, because he did not wish to discourage his friend.

"How old are you?" he asked.

"I just turned 34 last week."

"There is a chance then. The senior agent is pushing 40. Go for it! Practice! Join the gym; I recommend the one that Hassan goes to. It's a good place to learn. When you're fit and ready you can start looking for someone with power and influence to help you join the president's detail."

"Can't you guys propose my name?"

"No, we can't. It's not our province; but you can count on our goodwill, and that will do plenty for your appointment," Homero lied. He knew the agents did not have that kind of muscle.

"Thanks, pal. I'm counting on you already."

"No problem. Don't give up! Do as I say and you'll be halfway to your goal of being one of us."

Homero took his car for a test drive. As he drove along, he weighed the mechanic's request in his mind with thoroughness and care. At that point there were no openings. Even if there were any, the list of candidates favored by politicians close to the president was huge. The only other big shots with some power to make such appointments were Minister Lucio Fanzine and Lt. Col. Blake.

However amazed by the Arab's professional savvy, Deivid was filled with confident expectation of the fulfillment of his design. He thanked God for his keeping in shape by jogging six miles every morning: his only form of exercise. He had been running this routine for quite some years, although he was not certain as to how it could work to his benefit, except maybe his heart. He was sure of one thing, though: all that jogging would pay off, because it would provide him with the strength to learn how to fight like a Rambo. "And come tomorrow," he thought, "I'll start practicing my marksmanship at the target range on my brother-in-law's small ranch out in Taguatinga a ways." He would alternate jogging with target practicing. He owned a handgun and would have no problem getting extra bullets from the palace gunsmith whose car he also repaired out of sheer friendship. As for improving his fighting skills, Deivid intended to join the same martial arts academy frequented by Hassan as Homero had advised. He made a point to learn from Hassan's Arabian friend Gamal, with whom he practiced and was always chatting.

"One day I'll sure as hell be accepted as a part of that closed circle around the president even if I have to turn the whole wide world upside down."

Hassan left the palace and went straight to the gym. Inasmuch as he had been assigned to accompanying the president on a trip to Asia and Europe, he saw fit to let Gamal know that he would be away for a couple of weeks. After all, the instructor had told him that they would be delving into a few complex new-technique wrestling moves.

"You and your boss will spend all this time in the city of Sao Paulo?"

"Nope. This time around, the boss will visit a number of farms in the countryside of the State of São Paulo. From there we'll fly out West to see three more in Mato Grosso." "When you get back I hope you'll be willing and ready to learn these new moves. They're kind of toilsome and rough, but I'm sure you've got the hang of it by now."

The next day afternoon Gamal was a little surprised when a dark, strong, young man of median height came up and introduced himself as a friend of Hassan's.

"My name is Deivid. I'm a colleague and a good friend of Ibrahim Hassan's. I'd like to have a word with you."

"Why, sure! It's a real pleasure to meet you. Funny, but Hassan never mentioned your name."

"Well, you know the Arab. He's a tightlipped kind of guy, loath to speak about anybody or anything, even his closest friends."

"Do you also work with him. Same job kind of thing?"

"Oh, yes! Like I said we're colleagues. We're fellow members of the same profession. Only he is in one section and I work somewhere else. Our goals are pretty much the same, though."

"Why didn't you go on the trip out West to see the farms?" Deivid frowned, put both hands on his hips and said to Gamal:

"I'm afraid I don't follow you. Farms? What farms?"

"Hassan went on a trip with his boss. They're visiting some farms down South and out West."

"Are we talking about the same Ibrahim Hassan?"

"Sure! Ibrahim Hassan, my wrestling student."

"Hassan must've been pulling your leg." Deivid seemed puzzled. "Hassan and I work at the Planalto Palace."

"Say what? The presidential palace? Like where the President of Brazil hangs out?"

"You mean you didn't know? Hassan never told you anything?"

Gamal was quite taken aback, but he put forth a tremendous effort to look and sound natural, oozing shrewdness from every pore to come up with a reply that would not give him away.

"Oh sure. I did know all about that. I was just throwing a bait to make sure that you really are who you say you are. All kinds of people keep calling on me for an opening in one of my classes; and they invariably claim having a close friendship with high-ranking authorities and influential politicians, or friends like Hassan, and so forth. Well, you know, I'm a very busy man on a very tight schedule. They all want in on my timetable." That did not faze Deivid in any way.

"So there! Now you know who I am, and there can be no doubt that Hassan and I are great pals. I'm also looking for a breach on your schedule. Can you teach me how to fight?"

"I only teach wrestling."

"Doesn't matter. I need to be good at one category of self-defense at least. I really don't care which. Do I have a chance?"

"I'll have to look over my agenda and see if I can squeeze you in. For the time being you can fill in for Hassan while he's away. When he gets back, we'll see what can be done to make this thing work out."

"I'll go with that, but I don't want to rob the Arab of his class. After he lost his whole family in Iraq, these classes have been a balm to his loneliness, to put it in the words of Agent Carlos. Back at work everybody agrees that things are looking up for him. The classes sort of eased down the state of depression with which he had to contend. The pain was killing him."

Gamal just could not believe all that flood of startling information. So, that was it. Hassan was dealing with dour problems and never said a word about them. He was an emotionally feeble man; therefore an easy prey. He just might turn out to be a perfect partner. He needs to be worked on, of course.

Gamal decided to lead Deivid into saying more.

"That's right," he said nonchalantly. "I remember now he once mentioned in passing something about the loss of relatives in the Iraq War. I didn't encourage him to go into details. I've got enough problems as it is."

"It was serious, very sad indeed," Deivid went on. "The grandmother, the mother, the fiancée, they were all killed off by a wide-of-the-mark American bomb that fell on the hotel where they were staying. From that day forward Hassan became even more withdrawn which led to feelings of anxiety and depression."

All of a sudden Gamal found himself in a state of grace. Those were tidings of great joy. They would be extremely important in molding Hassan into a terrorist. Under the pretext of avenging their families, they would work as a team. Gamal could lie through his teeth by telling Hassan that he had also lost his brothers to the murdering Americans in Iraq. Together they would stage a historical act of annihilation. Those blessed revelations would come in handy; and as soon as he had learned everything Deivid knew, he would waste him. Hassan could never know about this conversation with Deivid. He could never know that he, Gamal, had got wind of his problems, his inner feelings. Distrustful as he was, Hassan would probably fade away.

Gamal seemed to be coolly unconcerned and indifferent. He wanted Deivid to leave with the impression that they were just making chitchat.

"It's always a great pleasure to meet a friend of Hassan's. Come back tomorrow at this hour! I'll spare some time to teach you the first moves. When he gets back from his trip, we'll see what we can do. Please, before you leave, don't forget to fill out the forms at the reception desk. Address, phone numbers, the works… House rules. Tell the girl at the counter that I agreed to take you on."

Deivid was cheerful and hopeful when he left. As usual, he had talked too much. He did not fear the Arab. As a matter of fact, he despised Hassan whom he considered a slow-witted, servile self-seeker who won favor by flattering influential people: "An abjectly submissive brownnoser," the thought. What Deivid did not know was that he was messing around with very dangerous people and putting himself into harm's way. He had no idea.

Gamal left the gym and sat on a step of the front stairs that led up to the mosque. He needed to arrange his thoughts in acceptable order and work out a plan to slaughter as many innocent lives as possible in an attempt to satisfy his insatiable, cowardly, stupid, and truly pointless religious hatred. Fanaticism is forever hungry and needs feeding.

Gamal knew that he had to kill Deivid before Hassan returned from his trip. He had copied the address off Deivid's file at the reception desk. After saying his prayers he would climb on his bike and, with the necessary caution intended to avoid notice, he would check out the neighborhood and locate the house. As soon as he deemed Deivid useless as a source of information, he would snuff out his life.

Deivid did not go to class from Monday through Thursday. He showed up on Friday. Gamal was frantic with worry, but managed to pull himself together.

"I thought you'd given up filling in for Hassan while he's away."

"No, nothing like that," Deivid said. "I came down with a head cold last week. I was laid up. Couldn't even go to work. Only today I feel well enough to do anything. Can we start?"

"Sure! Got your outfit?"

"Bought it yesterday."

The terrorist gave him a lecture on fights and fighters, told him about ethics, conduct and attitude considered as befitting participants in sports, especially fair play, courtesy, striving spirit, and grace in losing. Sportsmanship should always prevail.

"The first lessons are almost all about stretching," Gamal said. "You do need a good stretch before you start any physical activity."

No sooner did Gamal notice that Deivid had a hard time stretching than he fabricated an excuse for a break.

"Since this is your first time, let's take ten for a breather. I'm going to have some water. Want to come along?"

At the drinking fountain, Gamal put his cunning, well-oiled tongue to work:

"You know, Hassan's behavior marked by all that self-restraint and reticence makes me wonder about what kind of mysterious life he probably leads. Was he always like that?"

"Not at all! There's nothing secretive about it. It's more like a humdrum existence; all work and no play. His daily rut is so lacking in interest as to cause a normal fellow a hell of a mental weariness. He goes home from the palace or he comes here or he goes to the mosque to pray or straight to his boss's house to play with the boss's little boy; a kid about two years old. From time to time he rides all the way out to the lake and just sits there all by himself."

"How come you know so much about him? Did he or someone tell you all that?"

"I was worried about him after that tragedy; so I decided to keep an eye on him and followed him around a couple of times. I didn't want him to do anything stupid like taking his own life," Deivid lied.

Gamal's mind was boiling over in multiple thoughts: "This guy's lying through his teeth. He's been trailing Hassan on a regular basis. I wonder why he does that"

"Well, I guess your work-to-home-and-home-to-work life has to be quite uninteresting and tiresome."

"It is for me, to be sure. Hassan's life ought to be a lot better, though. After all, being one of the president's bodyguards, he keeps traveling all the time."

Another precious piece of info on the man. "So he works near the president. He's a frigging bodyguard," Gamal mused.

"How come you are not a bodyguard like him?"

"Because first I must comply with certain requirements, namely, you know, knowing how to fight, becoming a sharpshooter y otras cositas más," he summed up.

"Oh, so that's why you took up wrestling?"

"Any mode of fighting will do. I need to be able to defend myself and also to strike. You see, come October, there will be a big shindig in Rio de Janeiro to celebrate the signing of some agreement involving a truckload of countries. A bunch of presidents will be attending: Brazil, United States, Venezuela, Mexico, you name it. If I were one of the president's bodyguards I'd be a part of it, too. But I'm not. So for me it's home to work and back home again. How boring is that? To top it off, I live by myself. My parents own a small ranch in Taguatinga. My ex-wife moved to Belo Horizonte. My life sucks. I kid you not."

"I hear you. Living alone is very unpleasant."

"When I become a presidential bodyguard, I'll go hunting for another woman."

"Is Hassan going to this shindig?"

"Absolutely! He never misses out on anything."

However ravenous for more information, Gamal wanted to throw Deivid off his track to avoid suspicion.

"I am kind of disconnected from that kind of news. I can hardly remember reading anything about it in the papers."

"The word is out in the media now, but this thing was all planned out a long time ago."

They went back to the tatami. Gamal put Deivid through a warm-up, then moved on to some stretching before they got to the core workout. When Deivid was all in, Gamal called it a day.

"You planning on coming on Monday?" Gamal asked.

"Sure. We'll have three classes before Hassan gets back Wednesday night."

"Until then you'll take his place. Don't worry about it."

"See you Monday!" said Deivid cheerfully.

"Monday," muttered the terrorist.

Gamal taught two more classes before he went to the mosque for his prayers. As usual, he sat on the steps to think things out. "A celebration attended by the presidents of the United States, Venezuela, Mexico… Wonderful! That idiot said nothing about the venue or the time. Come Monday I'll yank it out of him. Monday night I'll send him straight to Hell".

12

Raquel and Mauricio wandered through the night, visiting nightclubs and bars in shady neighborhoods, wearing suitable attire to avoid attracting attention, hugging and talking slang like a couple of lovers who had had one too many; but they could get neither clue nor lead as to the terrorist's whereabouts. After pocketing a hundred reais Raquel had slipped to him, the informant told her that absolutely nobody with a face like that had ever been seen in that den of perdition and dereliction.

"This clown," he said pointing at the sketch, "don't look like the kind of drifter that would hang out around here. You know, we can spot a clod like that a mile away. He'd stand out like a sore thumb, and somebody would remember him if he had showed his ugly puss in these parts. He looks more like one of those crazy Arabs who like to shove dynamite sticks up their asses and blow Americans to kingdom come. A religious freak, to be sure. I've met a couple, but I don't like to be around them. Not safe. Besides, they don't eat pussy, don't fuck, don't booze up, you know, they're useless. Don't belong in our world, not by a long shot. You can bank on that."

For a dark-alley pub, nincompoop philosopher, the informant's point was well taken. The sway of rascality stamped on the bearings and fearful countenances of pimps, panders, thieves, muggers, kidnappers, and all kinds of thugs who roamed the night did not harmonize with the meaningless expression on that cryptic face.

Around four o'clock in the morning, mingled with staggering drunkards, among couples making out or exchanging caresses or insults or even slaps, Raquel and Mauricio flagged down a taxi. Unconsciously moved by an overwhelming magnetic attraction, they agreed that it would be a good idea to swing by Raquel's apartment for a nightcap. Both were slightly intoxicated when she opened the door and invited him in. The special mood created by the circumstances conspired to what seemed to be inevitable; but it was not to be. They were both emotionally insecure. She was a recent widow: her husband, a policeman, had fallen in a shootout with traffickers. Mauricio had been cheated on by his fiancée who eloped with an ex-boyfriend. Mauricio and Raquel carried on like professional police officers.

"What's your pleasure?" she asked.

"Club soda."

She was not surprised, and Mauricio drank up his carbonated water.

"I think it's beddy time for you, Missy," he said with a smile. "You need to rest. Tomorrow, I mean, later on this morning, we have a date at ten."

Mauricio bade goodnight and left. Raquel locked the door behind him and shut off the lights. She stood there for a while, motionless, in the dark.

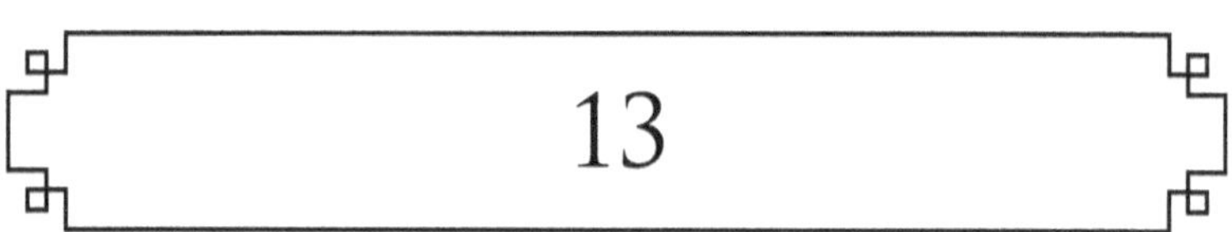

13

On Monday Deivid arrived early at the gym to make the most of the three classes he still could have before Hassan returned from his trip. He had to wait nearly one hour for his turn.

It turned out to be another terrible session of excruciating stretching.

"When am I really going to start learning how to wrestle?" he asked Gamal with a tone of anxiety in his voice.

"Only from the fifth session forward," was the reply.

"This stretching bit is boring and it sure as hell isn't motivating."

"Don't worry! That's how it should be done. You'll see how it'll come in handy when it comes to having to turn around fast to at once defend yourself from a blow and counterattack. If your body isn't in good shape, you may seriously distend a muscle and that will mean calling off any kind of physical exertion for a couple of weeks or longer."

During the break cooked up by Gamal they went together to the cafeteria. The terrorist carried on his routine of posing new and even more derailing and deflective questions with the veiled purpose of prying Deivid for more information about Hassan; every new piece of knowledge on the Arab was precious to him and he could easily commit it to memory. This time he learned the ceremony would be held aboard the Brazilian Navy aircraft carrier Rio de Janeiro on 15 October, and only a few guests would be in attendance. Stringent security measures would be enforced. Hassan was part of a select elite group that would be close to the presidents of Brazil, United States, and Venezuela. The others would be spread out all over creation.

Gamal was finally satisfied. He had completely drained Deivid of all the essential elements that would enable him to formulate a good plan; a plan he knew would have to be carefully worked out beforehand for the accomplishment of his gruesome objective. The night before he had ridden out to the Army housing complex and pinpointed Deivid's house.

When the stretching session was over, Gamal looked Deivid in the face.

"Good bye!" he said before turning on his heels and walking off without waiting for an answer.

Gamal went to the mosque, said his prayers, and headed on back to his hotel. He needed some time. It was almost two o'clock in the morning when he rode his motorcycle out to the surroundings of the Army housing complex. Carrying a backpack, sneaking through the dark, he pushed his bike towards the back of the house. At the backdoor he took a couple of tools out of the bag. He was so intent on unlocking the door that he froze in his tracks when he felt a cold, pointed, metal tip poke the nape of his neck and heard a hoarse voice whisper: "Don't move unless you want your brains scattered all over this here porch."

14

Mauricio moved stealthily over to Raquel's desk. She was deeply engrossed in her work, focusing on the computer monitor in front of her eyes. His "good morning" was barely audible. He silently pulled up a chair and sat quietly. Raquel did not seem to notice his presence. She kept moving the mouse around, apparently looking for something very important. She finally put it aside and turned her eyes to the Portuguese detective.

"Forgive me! Good morning!" she said. "I was so engrossed into reading up on the lists of cutthroats we have on file that I didn't notice when you sneaked in. I was trying to find an Arabian or any other foreign name that might hail from those parts."

"I didn't want to disturb you."

"Did you have a good night's sleep in whatever was left of last night?" she asked, flashing an enigmatic smile.

"Yeah, I guess! It was a passable night of rest. Yourself?"

"I managed to dose lightly."

"So, what's our next step, Madam Police Woman?" Mauricio said with a broad smile.

"I pulled up this Nasser fellow. Full name's Omar Nasser and another one, Jamil, Abdala Jamil! They both live in Santos and are suspected of giving shelter to illegal Islamic immigrants."

"What about the security cameras at the airports in Lisbon and Sao Paulo? Heard back from them?"

"Lisbon found nothing on their tapes. Neither did Sao Paulo. We're dealing with an expert here. He probably blended into the crowd, his head down, and got by without showing his face to the cameras; but we know for sure he was on that flight, because the Feds sent us a copy of the pic in his passport."

She handed the photograph over to Mauricio.

"It's pretty much what we saw on the police sketch. Nearly identical," he remarked.

"Well, I'm in possession of the addresses where we can find Nasser and Jamil. Let's mosey!"

"Your wish is my command!" said Mauricio as he got up from his chair."

Raquel did all the driving down to Santos, the well-known beachfront city in the State of Sao Paulo. They did not exchange a single word during the descent of the mountain road called Anchieta. They headed for the waterfront docks, the largest in Brazil, flashed their police ID's, and drove through the main gate. It was a quarter to noon. In fifteen minutes the siren would go off and all that state of extreme agitation and commotion of semis, trucks, trains, moving cranes, loading and unloading containers, would cease and all workers would take their lunch break. Raquel pulled over by a restaurant near Warehouse 17. They asked a few questions and learned that one of Arabs,

Jamil, had been killed less than a month before in a fight with a longshoreman. The other, Omar, had vanished into thin air. Rumor had it that he had moved down South and was now living in the outskirts of Paranagua, in Parana State.

"What now? Do we go there or get back?" Mauricio asked.

"We go back. Time is ripe for working out a refined search plan to find this terrorist in places where people of his persuasion like to settle down or hang out."

15

They returned to Sao Paulo. Gamal's face took on a shocked and horrified expression. He went into a paroxysm of terror, but gradually pulled himself together and cooled off when he saw who was threatening him: an elderly, lanky, clumsy, black man wearing a watchman's uniform. Gamal did not move while trying to come up with a good excuse for being in such an awkward situation. He needed to gain time.

"I was trying to unlock the door," he said raising his arms.

"No shit!" said the old-timer. "Well, I may be old, but not blind. You're a prowler trying to break in."

"No! Nothing like that!" — Gamal started to turn around ever so slowly — "I can explain. This here is Sergeant Deivid's place. He's a friend of mine."

"Keep your hands up. Let me see your face."

Gamal was now facing the old man. He noticed the soiled uniform and shabby cap on his head. Suddenly, Gamal was completely cool-headed.

"I forgot my key, is all. I'm a guest in this house."

The old man continued to hold him at gunpoint.

"I've never seen you in this neighborhood before. You're a goddamn burglar. You were fixing to break in and rob the sarge." The watchman waved his gun, pointing the way. "Come on! We're going to pay a visit to the cops."

"May I get my things first?"

"Sure. Take everything with you. Maybe you'll be able to explain to the constable that bag full of tools and the gloves."

As he turned to reach for his backpack, Gamal threw his right foot back with lightning speed and impact, kicking the old man's groin so hard that the zipper on his pants broke. The watchman dropped the gun, bugged out his eyes, and keeled over, cringing forward, shrieking from pain. In a quick move of thumb, index, and middle fingers, Gamal crushed his windpipe. The old man gasped for air and was dead almost instantly; an easy prey for a killer of Gamal's caliber.

After putting the gun away and picking the lightweight corpse off the ground, Gamal carried it on his shoulders into a thicket of bushes nearby. The night was dark. The street was badly lit. A waning moon barely allowed a glimpse of the buildings in the distance. He could not see a living soul.

Looking for a place to hide the body, Gamal came across a vacant lot where he found what was left of a well that went back to the days they built the city sixty years ago. He took the body and threw it into the well, waiting a couple of seconds to hear the dull thud of the fall. He felt a bit tired, having walked a good distance with the load on his back.

He rested a few minutes, and then he returned to execute his plan.

Gamal took off the latex gloves and thrust his fingers into a new pair. In two minutes he unlocked the backdoor with his special tools and slipped into the house. He stood there for a moment, listening for unusual noises and getting his eyes used to the darkness. Turning on a tiny flashlight, he stealthily inspected all rooms in the house. Deivid was sprawled out on a huge bed. Noiselessly he checked out the master bedroom and gently closed a half-open shutter which was the only opening allowing the entry of fresh air. He slid into the bathroom and quietly closed the door behind him. With the flashlight in his mouth, he used a wrench to carefully unscrew the hex nut attaching the gas pipe to the water heater thus releasing the gas into the atmosphere before it reached the heater. Silently he left the bathroom door wide open and closed the bedroom door. Without making the slightest noise, he got out of the house and locked the backdoor the way he had found it. He stripped off the latex gloves and put them in the backpack. He pushed his motorcycle as far as possible from the complex, then climbed on and ramped up onto the freeway.

As he rushed down the hall of his rundown hotel, he brushed by a hooker in blonde curls. He muttered a quick "Sorry" and rushed on to his room, but a sudden, rustling gush of a breeze brought back the woman's cheap perfume into his nostrils. Gamal's stomach turned over as if he had an urge to vomit.

He went straight into the bathroom, took a quick shower, and lay down in the dirty bed on his back with hands behind his head, staring at the ceiling. He could not help laughing when the thought came to him: "The police will go bananas trying to find out whether that clod committed suicide or not. And when they find the old man's body in the well, they will really freak out. It feels great to outsmart the fuzz. They won't have a clue to anything."

He fell asleep with a contented grin.

16

When the presidential plane landed at the Brasilia Air Base at 0500, A.M., [I recommend military time here.] returning from the tour Felipe Ferraro had made to Europe and Asia, the rain it was pouring really hard. That kind of The weather prevented him the staff from boarding the helicopter, as was the usual procedure.

The entire entourage went by car straight to the presidential palace, and there they would stay until the close of working hours.

It was well after seven when the president left the building followed by his staff.

Hassan was leaving his desk when the intercom beeped.

"Yes."

"Hassan?"

"Yes, Colonel,"—the boss's voice was downright unmistakable.

"Get over here!"

He reported to Blake on the double.

"Take my car and go back to the plane. Under my seat you'll find Guto's present. I forgot to bring it with me on account of that topsy-turvy deplaning."

When he heard Guto mentioned, Hassan was ready to start jostling.

"On the double, sir!"

He turned around and made for the door.

"Slow down, boy! Tell Lino to drive carefully. The roads are slippery. I'll be right here when you get back."— Blake smiled— "By the way, you're dismissed!"

Hassan got in the car and said to Lino, the driver: "Let's go back to the air base. There's a document I'm supposed to pick up. No need to speed like crazy, but step on it, will you?"

Lino smiled at the lack of congruence.

"I can't speed, but I have to go fast. Is that it?"

"That's about the size of it! Now move it! The boss is waiting."

Hindered by the usual, horrifying traffic jam in the rush hours, a situation that was worsened by the downpour which wouldn't let up, it took them nearly an hour to get to the base. Security red tape inside the perimeter pushed them back another half hour. Another hour to cover the way back, and it was nine thirty when they returned. Lino offered to drive him home.

"Thanks, but I prefer to go on my bike."

"In this heavy rain?"

"I got a special watertight slicker made special for bikers. I'll be just fine."

Knowing Hassan, Lino did not insist. He parked the car in the garage to wait for the colonel.

"I'll take this upstairs to the boss," Hassan said. "I don't think you'll have to wait long."

"No sweat," said Lino. "You guys were out of town all this time. All I did was sit around back here, gloating over the wonders of having absolutely nothing to do."

Hassan took the elevator, walked through several dark corridors, and finally arrived at Blake's office. Beams of light crept under the door and through the seams on the latch side, shining across the fine dust in the air.

As he reached forward and grabbed the doorknob, Hassan overheard strange noises coming from the inside. It sounded like a woman's intermittent moans of pleasure mixed with garbled, mingling voices and a man's primal grunts. He quietly twisted the knob and, with the door ajar, he stood there dumbfounded. A half-naked woman was lying spread-eagle on the colonel's desk, while Blake, pants and briefs down, stood between her thighs and pumped her with furious strokes; his white, harry buttocks stood out like a neon sign. As he slammed faster into her, she groaned and threw her head side by side with low cries of ecstasy.

Overcome with astonishment, Hassan could not take his eyes off the unfolding scene for a few seconds. Then he noiselessly closed the door and stood outside in the semidarkness, the package in his hand, without knowing what to do next. After a few minutes, his ears still pounded by the groans and grunts oozing out of the office, and with a flabbergasted expression on his face, he grumbled: "The bastard! Infidel son of a bitch! He is cheating on Dona Leticia, the most righteous lady I've ever met, so morally upright, so without guilt or sin…"

After a while, suddenly, all was quiet. Not a sound was heard. The moans and groans and grunts had ceased. Ten minutes later, the door flung open to reveal the colonel as he politely wished Celia, the minister's secretary, a good night. She vanished down the corridor; he looked at Hassan.

"Been here long?"

"No, sir! Just got here."

"Thanks," Blake said as Hassan handed over the package. "See you tomorrow!" he added, turning his back and closing the door.

Hassan walked to the elevator. Celia was nowhere to be seen.

"So it's that whore, the secretary," he muttered. "Blake is doing the bitch. It never crossed my mind that my boss was so vile. He lost my respect and my admiration. As far as I'm concerned he can die with the rest of the scum. That son of a bitch won't be missed."

That night Ibrahim Hassan could not settle himself to sleep. After drying off his motorcycle, he parked it on his porch, since he had no garage. He took a shower, donned his faded Bermuda shorts, and sat up late, watching TV. It was past two in the morning when he decided to go to bed. The scene of the colonel pumping Celia caused him to unremittingly undergo great mental anguish.

A grimace distorted his features, as he disgustingly reviewed in his mind that horrible scene; the groans and grunts kept pounding inside his head. He finally dropped off around five and slept until shortly after noon. He had been given the day off as a reward for the marathon of protecting the president for a whole week on a long journey.

In the evening he stopped in the mosque for prayers and went to the gym.

Hassan put forward a great effort to learn the moves that Gamal was trying to teach him. He did not accomplish much. At one point, after being easily laid out by the instructor, he stood up and stepped aside with hands on his waist.

"That's enough! Enough I say!"

"What seems to be the problem?" Gamal asked. "Are you alright?"

Hassan moved away from the tatami.

"There's no problem. I just want to call it a day. No more training for me tonight, is all," he said and started walking towards the locker room followed by an apprehensive Gamal.

"Let me help you, man!" Gamal said. "I can see you have a problem. Let's talk about it."

Hassan faced him

"Won't be possible," he said. "You have classes until ten, right?" "And your point is…?"

"Well, if you had the time, I would let you in on my problems. God knows I need somebody to help me get this off my chest. But forget about it. We can always talk tomorrow."

Gamal sensed the time had come. That was perhaps the only chance to yank anything useful out of Hassan who had been caught at a weak moment. He knew what he had to do.

"You were my last class tonight," he lied. "Yesterday, the ladder fell over while I was changing a light bulb in my bedroom. My shoulder is slightly injured"— he placed his right hand on his left shoulder— "I don't want to force it in any way. The assistant instructor will stand by for me."

Hassan and Gamal changed their clothes without exchanging a single word.

"Wanna talk to me?" Hassan asked, when they were ready to go. "Neither this place nor the mosque will do."

Gamal nodded his agreement.

"Where then?"

"Follow me!" Hassan said.

Together they turned and pumped their bikes out to the lake.

"What do you want to know?" Hassan asked after they got off their motorcycles by the shore of Paranoa.

"Is this your famous refuge?"

"Yes! This is where I like to relieve myself from tension or strain, where I take my ease, thinking about the sheltered life I've been leading, sorting out my problems."

"The name suits the spot, really does. Peace and quiet away from the city's hustle and bustle is all a man can ask for when he needs to get his shit together," said the terrorist, his arms crossed and eyes scanning the entire site with apparent curiosity.

"What do you want to talk to me about?" Ibrahim Hassan insisted with an impatient scowl.

Gamal walked over to the knoll, found a good spot and sat down.

"Come on over here! Relax! Take a load off your feet! You're too tense."

Hassan picked a spot and sat down next to Gamal who was now quite bold and ready to deliver his well-rehearsed harangue.

"My friend, I've noticed that you've been unsettled, very nervous and easily excited… and affected with sorrow. We are Muslims. We always pray together in the mosque, and still your uneasiness, this restlessness of yours, doesn't seem to let up. This goes against the teachings of the Holy Book. It is my sacred duty to help you. You would help me, to be sure, if the situation were the other way around. Tell me what is wrong."

"It's a long story," said Hassan without looking in his face.

"I'm here for you, my friend, and I'm all ears."

" "I caught my boss banging a secretary, that son-of-a-bitch infidel."

"Who, the president?"

Hassan blew up like a land mine. He sprung to his feet, shouting:

"Who the hell told you I work for the president?"

Gamal looked him in the face and opened a congenial smile.

"Take it easy, man!" he said. "The fact that you work for the president doesn't faze me any. I couldn't care less. Sit down!"

Still startled, Hassan refused to yield.

"You knew I worked for the president and never said a word to me about it? How did you find out?"

Straightforward and unemotional, Gamal crossed his arms, shook his head and, marked by calm self-control, offered an explanation:

"Hassan, when a new member enrolls in the gym, he tells the receptionist his address, home phone, work phone, the works. It follows that the staff runs a thorough background check on him. Large is the number of tricksters who cradle the dream of learning how to fight. Well, they make the first payment, delay and then default the other ones. Next thing you know, they simply vanish into thin air. Having a reliable file on our members is the only way we can cut down on our losses. Even so now and again we are cheated out of a lot of money."

Gamal cleared his throat.

"As far as I am concerned," he continued, "I really couldn't care less about your executive travels. It wasn't any of my business. One day, as I was going through my students' files with one of the gym owners, I noticed that you worked for the president of Brazil. Inasmuch as you are a forthright person, you filled out your forms correctly. You did not write Planalto Palace, of course, but you gave us their number. Well, that piece of information wouldn't add a single penny to my salary, so I didn't make much of it. When you came up with that tall tale of going on a trip as a secretary and errand boy for a rich business man I chalked it up to your desire not to affect an air of superiority as compared to us poor mortals by posing as the president's tough secret agent. To be honest with you, I admired you for that. I say again: you working for the president or any other top man won't fatten up my salary. I don't give a shit."

After a few seconds, his eyes riveted on Gamal's face, Hassan sat down. The terrorist held his gaze, and he looked away, picking up a stick off the ground and making drawings in the sand.

"Funny," Hassan finally said. "I never looked at it this way. I never thought that hiding my job from you would be considered humbleness on my part."

"That's why I've always admired you," Gamal lied through his teeth.

"Very well. In recent months my life has turned around big time. I lost my grandfather who was murdered by the rebels. My grandmother Harwah, my mother, and my fiancée Tsouli Raissa were killed by the Americans in Iraq…"

Hassan recounted all particulars of the tragedies that had befallen his grandfather and the rest of his family. He talked about his loneliness, the sadness of coming home to an empty house and his only joy left in life: Guto, his boss's son. He also gave Gamal a full report on his disappointment in Blake being caught in the act of adultery, on top of the minister's secretary. Hassan was consumed by a state of mental agitation and disturbance. He could barely hold in his emotions, and tears rolled down his cheeks when he finally broke down and came clean about assassinating the United States ambassador to Brazil in an act of revenge. That would be his rallying cry in the battle of life. Then he would shoot his brains out, and Raissa, his sweet bride would welcome him into Paradise.

Astonished, Gamal listened to him in silence without letting on his total disapproval of Hassan's idiotic notions. He had surmised that Hassan had serious problems, but not that serious… and culminating in a ghoulish plan of such proportion. The only motive in Hassan's heart was grief and a sort of helpless bewilderment at the thought of his terrible loss. He could be easily enticed into Gamal's plans. Measuring his words carefully, the terrorist expressed how sorry he was for all the distressing dark clouds that had settled upon Hassan's life. "But you, my brother," he said, "are not by yourself in your grim sorrows. I too have a sad story to tell."

17

In as much as their trip to Santos had rendered no fruits, Raquel and Mauricio concluded that, before going to Iguazu Falls, it might be worthwhile, as an acquittal of conscience, to search for Omar Nasser in Paranagua.

"Who knows? Maybe he provided safe haven to the terrorist?" she said.

"We'll know when we find him," he said out of politeness, for he sensed that Omar knew very little or nothing.

Raquel caught on to the subtleness in Mauricio's remark. She surprised him.

"I see eye to eye with you," she said. "Omar doesn't know squat; but then again we have to follow every lead, don't we?"

"I leaned that at the Police Academy," he said smiling. "I'm glad you read the same book."

"Not much difference from one country to another. Customs, culture, language… In our case, even the language is pretty much the same."

"When do we leave?"

"Tomorrow morning the van will swing by your hotel promptly at eight to take us to the airport. We'll be on the flight to Paranagua departing at ten-fifteen," she confirmed looking at the computer monitor.

They arrived in Paranagua around 1:00 P.M. and went from the airport straight to the police station. They asked about the whereabouts of Omar Nasser, whose record on the Sao Paulo police blotter read: "element of Arabian origin, unemployed and without a defined profession."

They were surprised to learn that Omar had been booked for vagrancy on the city waterfront. Omar had told the police he was just looking for a longshoreman, a friend of his, by the name of Luiz, but he did not remember his last name. This created reasonable suspicion by the police, but, since he had not committed any crime, they let him go. Omar liked to hang out in a modest eatery called "Arabias", frequented by his fellow Arabs.

Mauricio and Raquel found Omar having lunch at the Arabias.

"Nope! I've never met him," said Omar when confronted with the photograph. "He never looked me up."

"We are aware that you provide safe haven for Arabs if they can afford to pay you for your services," interjected Mauricio.

"I have been meted out a huge injustice by the authorities. This is a mistake, and I am a victim. I merely play out the role of guide. They come to me in search of a chance to find work, a cheap place to lodge, directions to find relatives and fellow countrymen. The authorities misconstrue my intentions. They call it safe haven to illegal immigrants and bandits… Well, if that's what they call a man who helps a foreigner to take the first steps in this country, then I plead guilty. I've lived in Brazil for 23 years now, and I still can't figure out the authorities."

"No money involved?" Raquel asked.

"Well, I need some sort of livelihood. Nobody likes to work for free. It's that simple. It's my means of support."

"You only work for Arabs?" Mauricio asked.

"Why not? Arabic is my native language, and the only one I know besides Portuguese. I'd be useless to anybody who couldn't speak Arabic."

"What if the person you're trying to help is a terrorist?" Mauricio insisted.

"How's a man to know? I provide them with the answers they need and help them to settle down. They pay me and I walk away. If they need more help, I'll charge them for it again. I don't make a secret out of it. It's my work."

"But not this one?" Raquel asked with her finger on Gamal's picture. "He never looked you up?"

"Not all of them look me up. Some go or used to go to Jamil who is, I mean, was my competitor. Few weeks back the poor, dumb bastard had an affair with a married woman and was stabbed by her jealous husband. He's dead."

"Do you know whether the man in the picture looked up Jamil?" asked Mauricio.

"No, I don't. We never exchanged notes on our clients lest we'd lose them."

"You and this Jamil were not friends?"

"Just acquaintances." I didn't trust him, and he didn't trust me. We exchanged formal greetings, nothing more."

"And I suppose there's no way you could help us find this man in the picture?" Raquel asked in a disheartened tone of voice.

"Maybe I could!"

Raquel's eyes lit up like wildfire. Mauricio pulled up his chair closer to Omar.

"Can you really help us?" Mauricio could barely hide his excitement.

Their great interest did not go unnoticed by Omar.

"What's in it for me?" he asked.

"Depends," said Raquel. If you know where he is, we'll buy your next thirty lunches and dinners in this restaurant, and we'll even give you some money to boot."

"No! I don't know where he is. I can provide you guys with a lead as to where he might've gone. No guarantee, though."

"If we think the information is worth anything," Raquel said, "even with no guarantee, we'll take care of today's lunch and dinner for you. Deal?"

"Deal!" said Omar.

"OK then! Let us in on what you know," she said.

"Quite a few Arabs go on down south to the Triple Frontier, a placed called Iguazu Falls…"

"I think we know that much," Mauricio cut in.

"Think again, detective!" Omar objected. "Some of them— Allah alone knows why— prefer this little village called Iasci not very far from Iguazu Falls and close to the Triple Frontier. I've always found this choice of venue rather strange. I've got a hunch that's the cat's leap."

"Cat's leap?" Mauricio looked puzzled.

"It's Brazilian slang," Raquel explained. "The cat's leap is the one move that is kept to oneself to be used only when it's absolutely needed. It's also the secret trick for getting something done quickly and properly. The secret is never revealed to anyone, since the cat's leap is supposed to be the element of surprise."

"Precisely," said Omar.

The couple looked at one another.

"Well, it is indeed a lead," Raquel said.

"Please call the waiter!" Omar exclaimed. "Pay him for my lunch and also for my dinner later on tonight. You guys promised. I've been down and out lately."

18

Gamal briefly directed his gaze at Hassan whose constricted face seemed to be accruing harsh ruminations.

The bodyguard took out a handkerchief and wiped away his tears.

"Knowing that you came from those parts," Hassan said, "I can only imagine the ordeal you've been through to manage to get this far out West."

Casting a lusterless glance at Hassan, oozing treachery from every pore, and masking his face in a deliberately misleading candidness, Gamal began to tell his story in his best deceitful drawl and with such a conviction that he himself was surprised at his blistering cynicism.

"I used to work in a munitions factory in a suburb of Baghdad. My only two brothers were kind, peace-loving people who owned a clothing store in the capital. One day, one of my brothers found a submachine gun that someone had left leaning on a wall in back of the shop. You know, one of those lightweight automatic guns you can fire from the shoulder or hip."

Hassan nodded.

"Well," Gamal went on, "he called our other brother, and they both picked it up and looked it over. It was a bait. You ever heard of 'the baits'?"

Hassan shook his head in absolute bewilderment.

"Let me tell you about it. American soldiers deliberately leave some sort of small weapon, usually a rifle, lying around where it can be easily spotted, like it was forgotten by someone who had to sally forth in a hurry. They call it 'a bait.' Well, then they hide and stake out the place. When an unwary victim touches the bait so as to leave fingerprints, they cut him down mercilessly. My brothers innocently fell prey to the trap set up by the Americans. When I heard, I was in utter despair, my heart aflame and my eyes blinded. I ran away from Baghdad, swearing one day to avenge the dastardly murder of my brothers by taking out at least ten Americans.

In a dramatic gesture, Gamal brought out a handkerchief and wiped his nose and face before he went on with his deceiving account.

"I had to endure all kinds of vicissitudes and shifts of fate before I ended up in Naples, Italy. I spent almost two years there, working at a fireworks factory near a wrestling gym where I took lessons and practiced in the nighttime. My salary was barely enough for me to eat, pay the rent and my way through the wrestling classes."

The truth was that Gamal had been sent to Italy to plan ahead for a terrorist attack that had to be aborted at the last minute, because no security breach existed to make it feasible.

After a drawn-out wait, he got his orders to move on to Macao for the purpose of learning Portuguese as far away as possible from the intense police chase on terrorists. Actually Gamal had become adept at martial arts and proficient with explosives and bomb-making in an Al-Qaeda training camp somewhere in Pakistan.

"And how did you wind up here?" Hassan interrupted.

""Well, I'll tell you. I'm very handy with languages. From Italy I came straight to Brazil," he said, leaving out his tours of Macao and Lisbon. "I lived in Sao Paulo for a good while, and I met some fellow Arabs back there. I borrowed money from them. I set up a stall and became a street vendor. Nice little thing about Brazil, isn't it? You can pull a stunt like that and get away with it without paying any taxes. I managed to pay off my creditors, but was pissed off at the high interest rates they charged me with no regard for a fellow countryman. How could I carry out my vengeance plan? Besides, Americans don't mess around in Sao Paulo. I mean not in large groups. It would be nearly impossible to take out a whole bunch of them in one strike. You can bump into droves of Jews, Lebanese, Italians and even Japanese in Sao Paulo, but a throng of Americans is hard to come by. Well, anyway, after two years, I sold off the stall, gathered up my stuff and headed out to Brasilia. After a very stringent examination I was hired as a wrestling instructor at the gym, and by dint of a great deal of effort I learned Portuguese, and now, as you can see, I'm pretty fluent and hardly have any discernible accent."

"Why Brasilia?"

"Did you know that the American Embassy here in Brasília employs a staff of more that seventy diplomats and that all of them are American?" Gamal replied right off the top of his head, inasmuch as he knew next to nothing about anything concerning the U.S. Embassy in Brazil.

"No, I didn't," said Hassan a little impressed.

"Well, let it be known then. Also, I intend to find a way to break into the Embassy and blow the greatest possible number of gringos to kingdom come. That's why I'm here."

"Are you a terrorist?"

"Who? Me? No!" Gamal was emphatic. "I'm doing it out of sheer vengeance, I mean, the infliction of punishment in return for an unforgivable wrong they have committed. You intend to take your own revenge by killing the ambassador, right? That doesn't make a terrorist out of you, does it?"

"That's right. I'm going to do just that. Are you also killing yourself in the process?"

"Do I have another choice? Well at least I'll take no less than thirty gringos with me."

Hassan just sat there in silence, scribbling on the ground with a stick. The story told by Gamal sounded weird, but it made sense. It was only natural to try to avenge the assassination of your brothers.

"Why haven't you done it yet?" he asked, facing Gamal.

Gamal got up on his feet, put his hands on his waist, and looked away as if searching for something in a far-off horizon.

"In one word, my friend: money. There is the rub. I need a considerable amount of greenbacks to purchase the raw material for an explosive device. As I said, I dealt with explosives. Once the ingredients are available, I can make a bomb with one hand tied behind my back. No problem in that department. Anyway, it's not just the bomb. The largest investment would be to procure an AR-15 rifle with enough ammo, or even an AK- 47. Those babies don't come cheap."

"Haven't you made enough money yet?"

"Not yet! The first step was buying the bike. The problem of getting around is solved."

"What are you going to do about the bomb?"

With a conniving look the terrorist lowered his voice.

"I have a friend in the Bat Cave Shantytown out near Tabatinga. He has connections with arms dealers. He can get the stuff. I've been saving the cash to close the deal. I've also made up a list of the things I need. The shanty people deal with the smuggling of weapons, explosives, and ammunition into Brazil. They're pros and say there won't be any problem. All I need is to come up with the dough."

Gamal was lying again. He had everything he needed ready and packed in a metal box, which he had buried in an empty lot near his hotel. He had acquired it through a prostitute who took customers to a room near his. She introduced him to a trafficker. Gamal paid a small fortune for his goods, but that was never a problem for him. He had come over to South America bearing a good bundle of money. He was just waiting for instructions as to where the bomb should blow up. He did not know what the intentions of his superiors were, but he suspected they might tell him to set if off in one of the houses of Congress or the largest mall in Brasilia.

It was not up to the bomb man, as was Gamal's case, to speculate what the Al-Qaeda high-command plans were. The only acceptable exclusion would be that if there arose a major favorable and advantageous circumstance or combination of circumstances offering a target of opportunity of mind-blowing importance. According to the bizarre reasoning of Gamal's radical chain of command, that might very well be the case for a suicide bomber to make the decision to carry out a strike and perform his self-sacrifice, carrying their blessing and justification with him.

Since he was totally engaged in the task of subtly imbuing Hassan with a fundamentalistic point of view, Gamal chose to mix lies with half-truths to settle his scores without scaring him away. If there were the scantest reason to suspect that anything said to Hassan had leaked, he would not dither from killing him and finding shelter in another suitable country on the continent.

After listening to Gamal's harangue, Hassan quickly leaped back on his feet and looked at his watch.

"It's getting late," he said. "I think we should mosey."

The terrorist did not answer at first. He just walked over to his motorcycle and climbed on.

"As you may have noticed," he said, "my shoulder is hurt. That will keep me off the tatami for a while. Wrestling school is out for you and me. We should meet up here tomorrow. I've just come up with a real honest-to-goodness brainstorm. Think you can make it?"

"OK. What's your good idea?"

"No, let's not talk about it now! Give me some time to weigh it in my mind with thoroughness and care. Tomorrow at, say, fivish?

Hassan nodded.

"You'll love it," Gamal said with a congenial grin. "See you tomorrow!"

He revved and sped off with the rear tire screeching.

19

Twice a week, in the morning, Dona Raimunda paid a visit to Sergeant Deivid's home. On Tuesday she would pick up his laundry and, on Friday, bring it back spotless, clean, and pressed. With a copy of the backdoor key, she went right in as usual and walked straight into the master bedroom where she expected to find his dirty clothes in a hamper.

She found it strange that the bedroom door was closed. By that time the sergeant should have long gone off to work, and he had never closed that door before. She knocked first and got no answer. She turned the knob quietly. It was no surprise that the door was unlocked. She went in and stopped two feet from the doorway. Sergeant Deivid lay in his queen-size bed facing the window in his underwear. The room breathed gas and death.

Dona Raimunda immediately felt extreme discomfort from lack of fresh air. Half-dazed, she stumbled out to the street, gasping for dear life. She thought of going back to the bedroom, but fear had the best of her. She rang the neighbor's doorbell and asked for help. "Mr. Deivid is in serious trouble!" she thought.

From that point on, things began to happen quickly, and the usual sequel followed: police, medics, and firefighters swarmed the housing complex. The street was a carnival of flashing spotlights on police cars, vans, and fire trucks. Secret agents arrived in a black sedan and took over the scene. In less than ten minutes Deivid's blanket-covered body was laid on a stretcher and loaded unceremoniously into the back of the coroner's black van. By the time the reporters got there, they found out very little about what had really happened, and the house had been cordoned off with police tape on both sides of the property and a squad vehicle stationed outside.

The presidential staff pulled some strings, and the case was mothered by the media from the public. The next morning there was nothing but a short note in only one newspaper: "Gas leak kills the lone resident of house 26 in the noncommissioned sector of the Army residential complex. The victim served in the Presidential Palace. Nothing was stolen. Suicide is suspected."

Back in the Palace, Commissioner Joseph Lavradio, deputy chief of the Department of Internal Investigations, was given the order to proceed to the scene of the "incident" accompanied by two detectives from the Homicide Unit and conduct a discreet and prompt investigation. Whatever the outcome, the final word would be up to a higher authority that had already established the cause of death to be suicide from gas inhalation.

To top it all off, Lavradio's superior Dr. Romualdo Sodre personally gave him specific instructions in his usual, elaborate display of affectation that emphasized gesture, vocal production, and delivery.

"There is no room for academic uncertainty or ambivalence in this case! Undoubtedly, this was a desperate act of a disturbed soul who intentionally took his own God-given life. However, for the purpose of complying with and showing devotion to the rigid, annoying minutiae of administrative procedure as per the law, have two investigators from the Homicide Unit accompany you, but by no means allow them to be excessively meticulous with all those fussy forensic techniques that just might astound us with the far-fetched possibility of a different conclusion. We cannot afford to expose any sort of fragility that will make the pillars of the operating structure of the Presidential Palace liable to danger, suspicion, or disrepute. A misinterpretation in an incident of this caliber may very well turn out to be a precious gift to our political opponents."

Dr. Sodre cleared his throat, stroking his mustache in sheer contentment at the pantomime which had enhanced his already overblown rhetoric.

"Do I make myself quite clear?" he asked, closing his peroration.

As a public servant, Lavradio had always known that the highest award for public officials in Brasilia was a billet at the Presidential Palace. He also knew how to play out his part and thereby hang on to his good, well-paid job: he was supposed to slavishly agree with his superiors. So he never paused in uncertainty before his answers.

"Perfectly clear, sir!" he said, but he thought otherwise: "I'm on to you, you pompous asshole!"

"So be off and take the appropriate action!"

It was not easy. Detective Romildo da Costa, known only as Da Costa, closely examined the gas heater and had no problem to come to a conclusion.

"Hey, chief, no way in hell it was suicide."

"Say what?" Lavradio's reaction sounded like a sure forewarning sign of trouble ahead.

"Take a look here, Chief!" da Costa said, pointing. "The nut was unscrewed from the bolt and the bolt withdrawn."

Controlling his rage, Lavradio pushed the detective aside and stared at the hex nut.

"Don't be an ass! That suicidal wacko took it out himself.

Da Costa was with the Homicide Unit of the Brasilia Police Department. He had no ties whatsoever with the Palace staff or any other branch of the Executive. He had been assigned upon request in compliance with the law that required expert opinion in possible murder cases. When ordered to accompany the president's people, he acted as the young, competent, motivated professional that he was, guided by the resolve to help. However surprised at Lavradio's boorish reaction, he naively remained firm in his course.

"Why would he do that? And where are his tools? If he really wanted to kill himself, why didn't he just flip open the gas switch, and why would he take the trouble of putting away his tools? How can I be wrong?

Da Costa's companion, Detective Luis, was used to backing up all assumptions made by higher authority, however unlikely.

"The chief is right," he said. "It was suicide."

Lavradio felt relieved with Luis's support.

"This case is closed. It was suicide."

He made that typical summoning gesture.

"Let's get the hell out of here!"

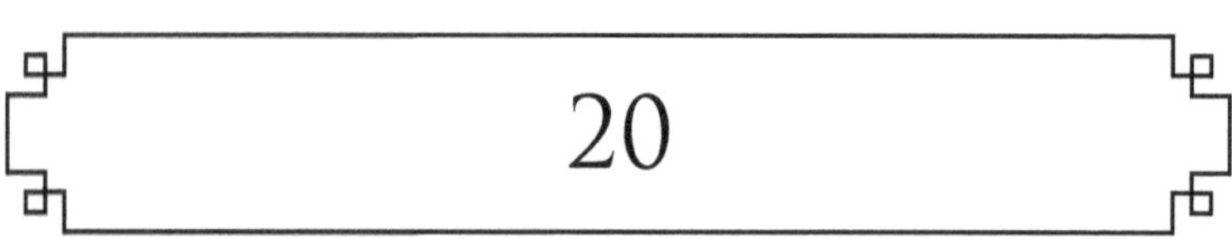

20

From Paranagua Raquel and Mauricio went on to Iguazu Falls on a shimmying bus along badly-paved roads, dodging potholes.

In The Falls they went straight to the hotel. They were both dead tired, so dinner was also at the hotel. After planning their detective work for the next day, they retired to their respective rooms.

In the morning, after breakfast, they walked over to the police station. Despite the goodwill of their local colleagues, they learned nothing new. No one recognized the man in the photograph. It was strange to them that the police were uninformed about the suspected presence of terrorists in that area; actually, their investigations were targeted only on issues concerning drug traffickers, arms smugglers, car thieves, and even bootleggers who traded goods illegally on the border with Paraguay.

They took a stroll through the city.

"Let's go on to Iasci," Raquel blurted out impulsively.

"Like now?" Mauricio showed his surprise.

"No! Like tomorrow morning. After breakfast, we'll dress like tourists and rent a car. We'll check into a nice hotel.

They arrived in Iasci shortly before eleven on the next morning. They drove around town looking for a suitable hotel. Finally at 2 p.m., they checked into the Astoria, situated on a quiet side street near the main thoroughfare. As directed by Raquel they acted like a married tourist couple who wanted a room with two single beds.

Mauricio sat on the edge of the bed by the window. He knew women usually preferred to stay closer to the bathroom and the mirror.

"OK by you if I grab this bunk?" he asked, apparently ill at ease.

Raquel did her best to sound casual. She smiled.

"Good choice! We women need plenty of leeway when we're getting ready to go out. Tell you what: let's not unpack now. We can do it later on tonight. There's still plenty of light out. Let's go out and do some serious police work while we take in the sights."

She realized their situation was somewhat awkward.

"Give me just a moment! I'll be right back!" she said before locking herself in the bathroom.

From the very first day they met until then, a very subtle energy of mutual attraction gradually took over their grief-crippled hearts, which had made them indifferent and insensitive to matters of the flesh as a result of the cruelty of fate that had caused them a great deal of pain.

Disappointment and woefulness had settled upon their lives in different ways, but the consequences were the same:

feelings of friendship, lust and passion had long been thrust aside; those were now part of a past of painful memories. From the beginning Mauricio and Raquel harbored the notion that they had hit it off purely on the basis of mutual congeniality and never realized how wrong they were. They were simply afraid to admit that they had fallen in love with one another and had a latent emotional affair going on; but the unforeseen became a reality in the seclusion of that hotel room. As Raquel came out of the bathroom, she tripped on one of the bags and lost her balance. Mauricio leaped up to prevent her fall and managed to protect her body with his own. They rolled end over end and wound up on the floor in a tight embrace and their cheeks glued together. Slowly they slid their faces until mouths and tongues fully met in a warm, sensual kiss. Bodies still clinging together, they rose from the floor and tangled on the nearest bed. They were incredibly quick to get rid of each other's clothes and leave them scattered all over creation. Then it was slow and sweet. They were naked, possessed with an intense eagerness, moaning in pleasure, quenching the pent-up yearning that had been repressed at the core of their until-then unconscious, unattended desires, overflowing with tenderness and unfulfilled love.

After deciding to stay in the hotel that night, they unpacked, sent out for food and drinks and pushed the beds together. They had sex again and again and fell asleep at 2 a.m.

They were up again at seven.

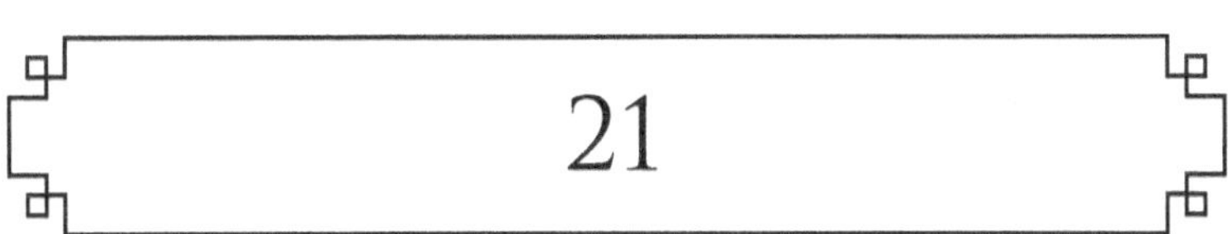

21

The next day, sitting in the refuge by Lake Paranoa, Gamal thought frantically for a way to lay out his plan to Hassan. When he heard the roar of the motorcycle approaching, he tamed his anxiety and remained calm.

Hassan pulled up close to him but did not get off his bike.

"Our talk has to be put off until tomorrow," he said. "Can't make it today."

"You came all the way out from the sticks just to tell me this?" Gamal said, barely concealing his vexation.

Hassan was in a bad mood.

"What else could I do? Your habit of never carrying a cellphone is a damn nuisance. Get smart and learn how to use one. Next time around, I won't bother to let you know."

Gamal clenched his teeth in an effort not to lose his temper.

"Well, do pardon me!" he said, letting his tone betray his frustration. "No way. I hate cellphones. Do you have a problem with that?"

"Well, I'm on my way to visit with the little boy, my boss's son. He's sick. He asked for me to see him."

The terrorist took a long breath. He couldn't believe his ears.

"Is it so important to visit with a kid?"

Hassan turned the motorcycle around and started to rev up and drive away slowly.

"You have no idea," he replied. "That child is the only human being I care for. I don't give a shit for anybody else in this stinking world. See you tomorrow at this time."

He drove off leaving a trail of dust and dirt behind.

An outburst of harshly abusive language flowed from Gamal's mouth in a crescendo: "The stupid idiot, the cretin, the jackass, the dumb-ass son of a bitch!" Gamal was furious, but Hassan did not hear him; he was far off.

The terrorist stood up straight away and patted the sand off his clothes, musing and mumbling: "This moron is a sentimental fool. Deivid was right. He's just a sycophant sucking up to the boss's son. Or is he really? Could it be that he really is fond of the boy? This is a typical case of a loner; a solitary, disoriented soul searching for someone to cling to… like emotionally. He is marked by memories of the children in that daycare center, where his woman worked. The boy is how he makes up for it, how he compensates. This guy is not normal. He's a wacko. Has to be. Manic-depressive, to be sure. Friendless, eager to fill the void of his loneliness by channeling his affection for the figure of a child who cannot hurt him in any way. Talk about inexplicable obsessions! What else could it be? Thanks to Allah the boy is unable to interfere with the plans I made for that dullard."

He climbed on the motorcycle and revved up.

"And here I am talking to myself. I'm just about as crazy as Hassan!" he said out loud before starting back for his hotel.

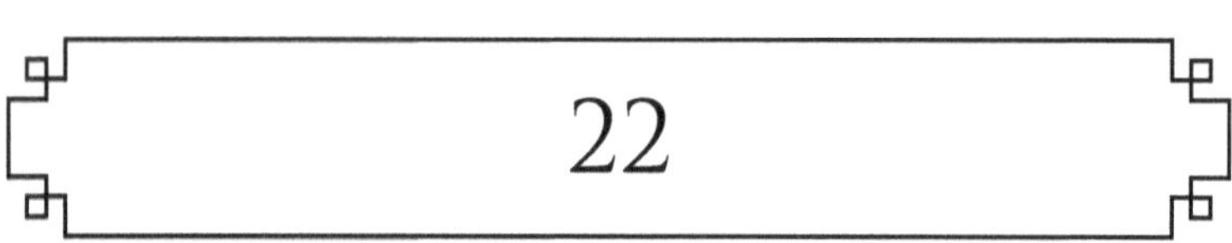

22

A problem came up in Lavradio's office, on the ground floor in the back side of the presidential palace. It is a wing dubbed "backstage," since it comprises the quarters and working places of lower-rank servants.

A one-page, run-of-the-mill report on Sergeant Deivid's suicide was ready to be initialed by the investigators. Lavradio was sitting at his desk; in front of him stood the two detectives. He signed the paper and slid it over to Luiz who repeated the gesture without even reading it. On his turn Da Costa took his time to read and re-read the document. He put it back down on the desk.

"Chief, I'd rather not sign this report. I beg you to excuse me, but I disagree with the conclusion," he said staunchly.

The commissioner turned red as the blood rushed to his cheeks. He stuffed his anger and, slowly, evenly, measured out his words:

"What is wrong with it?"

Da Costa took another look at the paper. He glanced at Luiz and there was no question about his companion's blithe lack of concern. Da Costa ignored him.

"A further, closer investigation, duly carried out by an expert, might very well determine whether it was suicide or murder," he said to Lavradio, who could not believe his ears and sat there in a state of amazement, his mouth wide open.

Lavradio stood up and crossed his arms over his chest.

"How old are you, son?" he asked.

Da Costa thought the question strange and to no purpose. He shrugged it off and his answer came almost in a murmur."

"I turned 29 last month."

Lavradio fixed his eyes on the detective in a solemn and thoughtful manner.

"I've been with the Force for 37 years. When you were born I had been a policeman for…"

The telephone rang out loud, cutting him off.

"Excuse me," said Lavradio, reaching for the phone. "I'm on my way!" he said into the mouthpiece and put it back on the hook.

"You guys just take a seat over there and make yourselves comfortable!" he said, pointing to the couch. "Be back in a jiffy."

He left the room in a hurry. The two detectives sat side by side in a pregnant silence broken only by the soft jumble of voices coming from the hall outside.

Lavradio stepped off the elevator and went straight into Dr. Romualdo Sodre's office. The secretary waved him in. His boss was on the phone. He started to leave, but Sodre gestured him to stay. Lavradio stood in front of an oil painting and pretended to regard it with pleasure, wonder, and approval.

Sodre hung up.

"Afternoon, boss!"

"Good afternoon, Jose!"

Sodre addressed subordinates by their first name to give the false impression there was a component of friendliness in the relationship. He felt it was a thoughtful display of concern, solicitude, high regard, and esteem. Lavradio had no illusions about that. He had his boss figured out from day one: he worked for an overbearing, arrogant, boastful, artificial, arbitrary, and imperious old man who asserted his authority and imposed his will in a highhanded, peremptory manner, expecting unquestioning obedience. Sodre tended to be oppressively and rudely domineering. His opinion was beyond challenge.

"I'm ready for my orders, sir."

"I would very much like to know whether you have already finished up the investigation on the insane act of that enlisted man and, if at all feasible, be informed as to the whereabouts of the respective report."

Lavradio was thinking: "What a pompous ass!"— But he phrased his words differently.

"It's almost ready, boss. I'm having a little problem with processing the paperwork, I mean, with getting all the signatures on it.

"I see. We have a dissenter, huh?"

"Sort of, sir. One of the detectives insists on a further, huh, closer inquiry into a few details."

"And what did you do?"

"Oh, this issue has just come up, sir. I was trying to talk him out of it when you called. The report is OK by the other detective, I mean, he raised no objections."

"What is the troublemaker's name?"

"Da Costa. Romildo da Costa. He is young and still full of motivation. His conduct is influenced by ideals that often conflict with practical considerations. A dreamer…"

Romualdo reached for the intercom as he wrote down the name on a piece of paper. He told his assistant to get the Secretary of Homeland Security on the horn. Then he turned to Lavradio.

"Okay, we settle this right now."

Lavradio made a hurried movement to leave the room, but Sodre stopped him.

"Stay. Wait until I talk to the secretary and see how this thing turns out. By the way, it may be a good idea to have the Maintenance Division replace the gas piping and all the heaters in every house on the complex, just in case. Speak to them in my name. I realize it is not our province, but we all must work as a team. I will provide a budget for expenses."

"Yes, sir. I'll see to it."

The interphone buzzed. It was the Secretary of Homeland Security, Dr. Paulo Henrique.

"Here's hoping all's well with you, my friend, and your lovely family!" Sodre boomed.

After the usual exchange of polite greetings and buoyant platitudes, Romualdo Sodre apologized for availing himself of His Excellency's friendship and inconveniencing him for a favor. "Not to me, of course, but to the president himself… You, my friend, understand that it is not always pleasant to make certain requests, but it is of the utmost importance… You know the Malagasy— or is it Corsican?— saying that goes 'one hand washes the other and both hands wash the face.'"

The bottom line was that detective Romildo da Costa of the Homicide Division was to be transferred to Narcotics, effective the day before. No questions asked. No direct or indirect expression of censure or discredit or any reflection whatsoever on the boy's integrity.

"You know, my friend, these requests from the presidency are difficult to circumvent… or explain," Sodre said, closing his argument.

One last exchange of courtesies, and the phone was back on the hook.

"Alright, Jose!" Sodre exclaimed in a weary, patronizing tone. The boy is no longer required to sign the report. Effective yesterday he has no business associated with the affairs of the presidency. If he insists, he will be summarily dismissed from the Public Service for insubordination."

"Thank you, boss. Am I dismissed?"

Back in his office, Lavradio was feeling sorry for Detective Da Costa. The Narcotics Division was nearly a punishment for someone who had specialized in homicides.

Dismissed by Lavradio, the two detectives went back to their headquarters. Da Costa, surprised at his appointment to Narcotics, never understood why his immediate boss would not even receive him when he requested an explanation. "Being first in my class in the Police Academy didn't help me any," he mused dishearteningly.

Alone in his office, Lavradio was still astonished at Sodre's arbitrariness.

"That man," he muttered to himself, "is cruel, insensitive, autocratic… He's also a braggart… A monster, that's what he is… in sheep's clothing."

23

It was their third meeting at the refuge. Hassan sat down on a pile of sand.

"Can we talk tonight, or do you have another pressing engagement?" asked Gamal, standing in front of him.

"Take a seat over there," said Hassan as he pointed to another mound of fluffy sand across from him, ignoring the question, "and explain your mysterious plan to me. I'm curious."

Gamal sat down leaning back on his arms and stretching out his legs.

"Does your plan still hold for shooting the American ambassador and then put a bullet through your chest?" Gamal asked.

"I never said what I would shoot. I wasn't sure, but now I know. I'll aim at his head point blank. Then I'll shoot my own brains out. Safer that way. You really wanna know? Yes, I've made up my mind. I'm gonna do it. There's no turning back. Why do you ask?"

Gamal savored every one of Hassan's words and it took him a few seconds to open his mouth.

"I've got a better plan."

"You do? A better plan?" Hassan sneered. "Well, go ahead then! Lay it on me!"

Just then an abrupt rush of wind blew off the lake, and they instinctively covered their faces with both hands to protect their eyes. It was sudden and quick. Again the refuge became an oasis of peace, calm, and tranquility.

Gamal's brain was boiling over with that lack of certainty that often leads to irresolution. Should he go straight to the point at the risk of an unpredictable reaction from an unstable man like Hassan? Or maybe he ought to avoid confronting the subject directly by using arguments that would arouse roguish feelings of sheer hatred and other negative emotions, thereby undermining Hassan's possible recalcitrance to a docile acceptance of Gamal's diabolical scheme. The terrorist chose the latter course of action.

"You will agree with me, as soon as you realize how simple it is," Gamal said, looking away as if searching for the right words. Then he looked in Hassan's face and added: "First let me ask you a couple of questions the answers of which…"

"Let's cut to the chase. What is your plan?" Hassan seemed to be losing his patience.

"Take it easy! Chill out!" Gamal said, gesturing with his arms to emphasize his words and thinking: "This guy is crazy."

"You'd rather kill the pilot of that plane that blew up that hotel and murdered your family, wouldn't you?"

"Sure! What kind of stupid question is that? What are you driving at?"

"Listen up, Hassan! That guy was complying with orders from his commander-in- chief. There is a chain of command that links him to the head honcho in Washington, who, in fact, is the only one responsible for all the tragic misfortunes that razed that part of the planet where Iraq is located. Who is this person?"

"Everybody knows that. It's the President of the United States. Funny you should ask me that. Do you take me for an ignoramus?"

"Hassan, focus! He is the man you have to kill by setting off a bomb near his ass. The bomb will kill both of you and there it is: the best way to get your revenge." Gamal pronounced these words with final, conclusive, decisive utterance.

Hassan was stunned. He stood up, beating the sand off his pants.

"No, no, no! Are you crazy?" he asked, staring at the terrorist with incredulous eyes and a livid face.

Gamal allowed some time for the message to sink in. Then he spoke softly, slowly…

"You can blow the president to kingdom come while he is signing that paper on the carrier."

Twice did Hassan unhurriedly pace back and forth with hands on his hips, staring into the night. He looked down at Gamal, who was still sitting, and took a long sigh.

"Unthinkable! Nothing doing! No way!" he said.

The terrorist kept his composure. He remained silent, waiting for Hassan to fully absorb the impact of his words.

"You know, when this notion popped into my head for the first time, I had a reaction just like yours: unthinkable, it cannot be accomplished, an impossible goal, unacceptable… Then, after carefully weighing the pros and cons, little by little, I realized how feasible it really was."

Gamal paused and remained silent for a few seconds, thinking: "In a drama, this is known as a pregnant pause."

"You see," he went on, "in view of your proximity to the president, it will be a cinch, a piece of cake. Think about it. You'll be able to punish the actual culprit charged with the crime of murdering your grandfather, Dona Harwah, Dona Tsouli and your beloved Raissa."

Gamal enunciated each name in distinct, meaningful syllables, expressing himself clearly and effectively. He wanted to rekindle and intensify Hassan's animosity and hostility towards Americans in general and one American in particular. As a result Hassan was stupefied with astonishment at such a display of a highly-developed memory.

"Amazing!" He exclaimed. "I only told you their names once."

"It was enough for me," Gamal said smiling gently. "I like to think that I have absolute control over my mental faculty of retaining and recalling facts, dates and names when they interest me."

"You were saying that my being near the president would make it easy to carry out my vengeance…" Hassan started saying.

"You are going to be near him throughout the ceremony, aren't you?" Gamal broke in.

"Sure! Near the Brazilian president."

"Isn't he going to be close to the American president?"

Hassan was startled by this question.

"Now wait a minute! Let me see if I got this right. In order to carry out your plan I'll have to kill our president, too? Is that it?"

Again Gamal didn't give him a direct answer, but spoke ever so softly.

"Are you close to President Ferraro? His friend maybe? Did he do anything at all when he heard about what happened to your loved ones?

Again Hassan paced the small stretch of beach back and forth with hands on his hips, gazing out at the lake with a taut expression on his face.

"Nothing! He did nothing of the kind," he said finally.

"What do you mean nothing? Didn't he at least commiserate with you or present his condolences in any way? He never said how sorry he was?"

"Never! Never did he bring up the subject. Sometimes I wonder if he knows anything about it."

"Come on, Hassan! You've got to be kidding, right? Everybody knew about it. It was all over the papers. You know how the media here always place emphasis on this kind of thing when there are Brazilian citizens among the victims."

"True," Hassan murmured.

"I didn't even know you then, but I remember reading about it and seeing it on the evening news," Gamal lied. "How can anybody in his sound mind believe that the president was the only one to overlook the whole thing?" Nobody in his sound mind will believe that, save someone simple and credulous as a child, which is not your case, my friend. I know you're not naïve, and maybe you're just trying to protect your president, uh, out of force of habit possibly; but deep down you know very well that Mr. Ferraro is a freaking infidel… cold and inhumane like any other infidel. Forgive my French, but that son of a bitch doesn't give a shit about you, even knowing that you are always there to cover his ass at the cost of your own life if it needs be," Gamal said excitedly.

There was another pregnant pause. And now, again, he spoke ever so softly in his best, elocutionary way.

"You know what, Hassan? Maybe if you were an officer and not just a lowly corporal, your president might have had a different attitude. Don't fool yourself, boy!"

Ibrahim Hassan froze on the spot and, arms folded, fixed his gaze on the nothingness in front of him as Gamal's jeremiad resonated in his mind over and over until it sank all the way in. Deep sorrow mingled with disappointment was stamped on his countenance. He was suddenly aware that he had taken notice of the president's unmindfulness from day one, but he, Hassan, refused to accept it and fooled himself with dumb excuses, scared as he was to face up to the harsh reality. Then, as if by magic, sadness and frustration faded away to be instantly replaced by sheer, intense hatred, the worst kind of hatred, the cold, calculating kind, the detached coolness that meant he did not care anymore.

Gamal watched all this with concealed delight and a thrill of contentment. He had managed to reach into Hassan psychic innards, but he never gave his ecstatic feelings away. He calmly rose, wiped the sand off his pants, and averted his eyes from Hassan's face. He stood there, waiting.

This time a stronger gust blew in from the lake and whipped through the refuge, forcing them to turn their back to protect their faces from the blast of sand. They had to hold on to their motorcycles to keep them from being toppled.

"It's getting late, and this wind's getting too damned wild. I'm getting the hell out of here."

"What about my plan?" Gamal asked.

Hassan climbed on his bike.

"Tomorrow, 5 p.m., right here," he shouted before riding off.

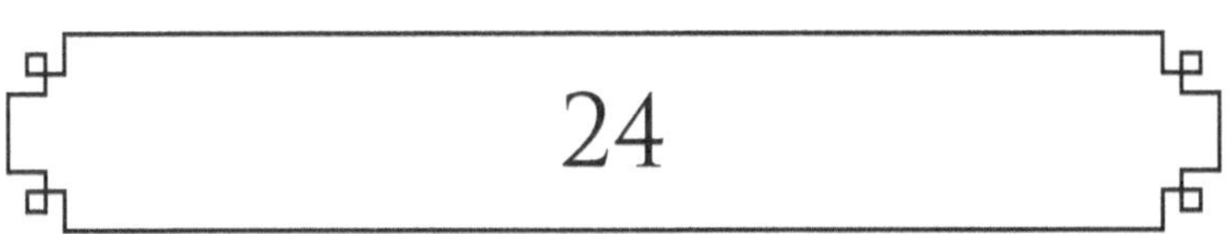

24

Raquel and Mauricio had breakfast at the hotel and went back to their room. She pulled up her e-mail on the laptop.

"My boss is really efficient," she said. "He put out a search for the terrorist in all the Interpol's 188 member countries and alerted the police of all the states. Since Brazil has no law that seeks the arrest or provisional arrest of wanted foreigners with a view to extradition, the so-called 'red notice,' he also notified the Ministry of Justice and the Supreme Court. They've already issued a warrant for the arrest of our man."

"Do we need that warrant?" Mauricio asked. "Isn't the red notice enough?"

"No, not yet. A bill is moving through Congress right now that will make this type of custody legal as in other countries. The United States is pretty much like Brazil in this matter, except that there any federal judge can authorize the arrest within minutes."

"So it follows that, if the police do not request a warrant in a situation like this, even bin Laden could roam the streets, and nobody would have legal cause to lay a hand on him, right?"

"Precisely. The police would be abusing their authority. They could get in big trouble."

"No offense, but we should applaud the judiciary system of my Portugal. We shrug off all that red tape. All we need is for the Interpol to put out a red notice and the wanted criminal is as good as arrested!" Mauricio remarked with a self-satisfied smile.

"Congrats!" exclaimed Raquel, concealing her frustration. "The first world is always a number of steps ahead of us."

"We're now ready to lay our hands on that terrorist," said Mauricio. "What next?"

" "Let's go out and walk the streets. We'll visit some hotels and other places in search of leads."

They went from place to place, claiming to be agents from an insurance company. They showed the photograph of the terrorist to no avail. They went to every hotel, inn, motel and bed-and-breakfast in town and all they got was: "Sorry, never seen him before."

On the second day, they visited the bus companies that ran the lines between neighboring cities. Department stores, tour agencies, everywhere; nobody had seen the man in the picture.

As they passed in front of a small factory that sold stringed instruments, Mauricio, a guitar aficionado— it was his favorite hobby— wanted to ask about a guitar on display.

The luthier was an old man who had a small shop in the back of the factory. Raquel showed him the photograph. They were surprised at his reaction.

"Sure! I've seen this man."

Mauricio and Raquel exchanged looks and their eyes went wide, darting back and forth, setting off their eagerness.

"Are you sure?" she insisted.

"Look closely. This is very important to us!" Mauricio exclaimed.

"I'm positive. One day he came by and asked if we sold harmonicas. Now that was a strange question, because the sign outside reads "stringed instruments." I told him we had guitars, violas, mandolins, and ukuleles, but not harmonicas. Then he asked me for directions to get to the interstate bus station. Well, I said that depended on where he was headed. He didn't want to tell me. He said he just wanted to know where he could catch a bus. Well, I said, if you're going to any of the neighboring towns, just go down this street five blocks and hang a left. He then finally said that he wanted to go out west to Brasilia. Well, in that case, I told him, you'll have to go to Iguazu Falls. The bus leaves from there. He thanked me and hurried out. I found it rather strange, because he never asked me where he could buy a harmonica. I don't think he really wanted one. Why are you looking for him?"

"We work for an insurance company. He collected the insurance for his stolen car. The car has been found. We need to clear up a few points."

"Are you buying this here guitar?"

"Not at this point. We're still trying to tackle a couple of problems on behalf of our company, and there's no way I can carry it around with me now. I promise to come back here, though, just as soon as we get this finished up."

The luthier pretended to believe him and wished both a nice day.

Back in the street the police couple, bursting with excitement, came near to falling into each other's arms so great was their joy. Mauricio gave her his arm and they walked into the nearest bar and sat at a secluded table. They ordered pop.

"What next?"

Raquel wiped her face gently with a silk handkerchief before she answered.

"First I need to settle my nerves and fight down the adrenaline. What about you?

What do you think?"

"I don't know. Wouldn't it be better to look into it a little further just to make sure?"

She looked straight in his face.

"I was thinking the same thing."

The sodas were served in giant glasses. They made a toast to their achievement, gulped a couple of sips and sat there gazing at each other.

Mauricio looked at his watch and broke up the silence.

"We still have plenty of time before this day is out. What say we hit a few more places and show this picture around?"

"Great idea! Let's go back to that little factory and ask for directions to a shop where one can buy a harmonica."

Mauricio waved down the waiter and paid for the soft drinks. The luthier let them in on a number of stores where they could find a variety of instruments including harmonicas. They checked out of the hotel and traveled back to Iguazu Falls. They still had some daylight left, so they mingled with the crowd and wandered about in the city. They entered into a store named "Empire of Sounds," a unique establishment. Nobody there had seen that man.

"Let's go back to Iasci," Raquel said. "We forgot to visit a very important place: the motor lodge. Every small town has at least one. They're discreet, muffled places, way off the beaten track where anybody can check in with no questions asked or picture ID's needed. Ideal for those who have to travel incognito."

25

Around four o'clock in the afternoon, near the Army residential complex, a group of youths were playing soccer on a vacant lot, when the ball was kicked out of bounds, winding up at the bottom of a well. A boy ran to retrieve it. He stood leaning on the edge of the pit and could see the ball nestled in the arms of what was clearly a human body. He called out to his friends and, in less than two hours, a small crowd of onlookers, firefighters, and police officers formed a circle around the corpse of an elderly black man lying on the grass and giving off a foul stench. With a sobbing gasp, a beautiful, young mulatto woman threw her arms about the thick neck of a sturdy, gruff-looking black man and cried convulsively.

This time there was nobody from the Palace to claim the body and remove all incriminating traces from the crime scene that might bring any sort of political damage to the government in the eyes of public opinion. Chief Joseph Lavradio, head of internal investigations, and his immediate superior Dr. Romualdo Sodre took notice of this piece of news through the newspapers.

"Do you think it could be linked to Sergeant Deivid's suicide?" asked Lavradio.

Sodre was his usual surly, peevish self.

"Suicide is one thing, murder is quite different. Let's not mistake the one for the other by establishing a connection between two incidents so far apart. I don't want to hear anything else about this. Do I make myself clear?"

That was enough for Lavradio. He buried all his doubts and drew on his resolve never to bring up the subject again. He apologized and exited back to his office.

Detective Marcelo Moreira was the agent assigned to the case. He was stunned at the beauty of Jandira, the lovely daughter of the deceased. He was bent on gaining her affections during the investigation. His motivation was boosted when told that the man on whose shoulders she had been weeping was just a good family friend. He accompanied her home to ask her a few questions.

The next day he paid a visit to the morgue and told her he would be back on Friday with the results of the autopsy. Jandira said that her father, Jose Ignacio, the night watchman, was a government employee and had been standing guard at the residential complex for more than five years. His salary was ludicrous, and he had virtually been neglected by a management that had failed to supply him with new uniforms. He was down to the last wearable one, which was drab and all patched up by his daughter. He stuffed his shoes with newspaper to cover holes in the soles and his socks were filthy from months of grime on them. He had no vices of any kind. He had been a widower for eleven years and led a quiet, sheltered life. He lived with his daughter who worked as a financial clerk in an appliance store. Marcelo and Jandira talked for almost two hours, and he promised to be back on the next evening. He still needed to clear up some loose ends. Jandira nodded and they said good night.

Back in the homicide division, Marcelo inspected the items found with the body that had been collected by the forensic technicians: an identity card, a ten-real bill, and a holster rig with no gun. Thinking more of Jandira than the work before him, he decided to go about it as slowly as possible, so that he would have a good excuse to spend more time with her. He had been so desperately attracted to her since he saw her for the first time near the well that he would not let a single day go by without calling on her to keep her posted on the course of the investigation. He told her about his suspicions, but always left out something suspenseful for the following day.

On Friday, the coroner reported that the victim had died of asphyxia by strangulation, the hyoid bone was fractured. Thus Marcelo had another good excuse to see Jandira and tell her that her father had probably been murdered. Anxious to impress her, he invited her to dinner at the modest restaurant on the block where she lived. Adding the usual exaggerations, inventions and fanciful stories, Marcelo, little by little, won over Jandira's heart and her love. He told her that her father was liked by everybody on the complex, because he was always so mindful of other people's needs. The families felt safer when they heard the night watchman blowing his whistle periodically in the night to scare thieves away. And so Marcelo's scheme to secure Jandira's admiration and affection worked like a charm. The girl was deeply impressed by his dedication, competence, police skills and, most of all, by his exquisite manners and tenderness. Jandira was taken in by all that power of pleasing and delighting, which hindered her good judgment and kept her from having the slightest doubt about Marcelo's character. She could not know how wrong she was.

He spoke low, but his voice carried far. He knew how to conform his speech to a certain proportion, adjusting pitch, intensity, and tone to the occasion. Because of this smooth-talking ability he was dubbed "Sweet Lip" by fellow policemen. This talent also concealed a cruel, cold, crafty, resentful, and vindictive temper. A self-explanatory example of his distorted morals reflects the pattern of his collective character and nature, out of which those destructive impulses grew up. It had happened ten years before when he arrived in Rio de Janeiro from his homeland Campina Grande, Paraiba State, and got a job as janitor of a small apartment building on Igarapava Street in the sophisticated neighborhood of Leblon. He was actually replacing his brother who had decided to go back home and suggested his name to the resident manager. His chores in the eightapartment building were simple and gave Marcelo time to study. He enrolled in a public adult-education center.

With persevering, painstaking effort and a great deal of quick-wittedness, Marcelo was soon prepared to take an aptitude test for middle-level public service. At that time he met a schoolmate, Linda, short for Lindalva, a luscious brunette with shapely legs, a trim waist, rounded hips, and perky breasts who lived in the nearby Vidigal favela. She was a manicurist at a beauty salon on Dias Ferreira Street, in Leblon. Alone and friendless, living in the confined spaces of the tiny janitor's bed-sitter at the back of the building's garage, Marcelo had nobody but Linda to hang around with or keep him company. It turned out as expected. They fell on love. Marcelo proposed to Linda.

Leading a suffocating existence, confined within a single-room shanty with a sick mother and three younger brothers, barely making do by earning enough money to buy clothing, food, and medicine for her mother and siblings, Linda did not think twice and said "yes." They got married. Fate had it that love was unable to develop its harmonizing power in a complete union, since this symbiosis of two bodies happened to be an association between souls of different species that could never benefit from one another. In a nutshell, Marcelo had boldness of enterprise, initiative, and aggressiveness to make it in life, and he needed money; Linda was trifling and frivolous, spent wastefully or extravagantly, and she lacked good sense.

One year later, Marcelo met Stenio, a good-looking, single bank manager whose hobby was hang-gliding. He made friends with the yuppie. From that day forward Marcelo raked in some "extra" on the side by taking care of Stenio's hang glider during the week, washing, mending and rigging it to be used and reused on weekends and holidays when Stenio would take off from Pedra Bonita ramp located in the Tijuca National Forest, Rio de Janeiro.

Inquisitive and prying, consistently keeping her own interests in mind, always when her husband's attention was diverted, ever so subtly, guided by her atavistic rules of eye contact, flirtatious glances, and innuendos, Linda got closer and closer to Stenio. Then, one afternoon, Stenio decided that his flesh was too weak to resist her tantalizing wiles. They wound up in a motel room and eagerly enjoyed the mutual pleasures of carnal knowledge. As time went by, as illicit lovers are wont to do in the course of an affair, Stenio and Linda began to ease off on the necessary precautions to protect the secrecy of their close-knit relationship. Certain that their arrangement was foolproof, they both failed to exercise the degree of care considered reasonable under the circumstances. It did not take long for Marcelo to realize what was going on between his unfaithful wife and their treacherous friend. The lovers were so confident in their ability to outwit Marcelo by cunning, artful handling of their rendezvous, often marked by scheming and deceit, that, on the assumption that he was out of the building on an errand, they set up a tryst for the next day while still in the garage, not knowing that Marcelo was also there under a resident's car, fixing a malfunctioning brake booster. Marcelo heard their faintly whispers and learned that they would meet in front of the beauty salon and drive up to the seaside VIP Motel, which was not far off.

On Friday, when he came home from work, Stenio saw that Marcelo was fitting out his hang glider. They chatted about trivialities, work, and dreams. The janitor mentioned his wild fancy to try a hand at hang-gliding. Stenio immediately offered to take him up on the upcoming Sunday. He even suggested that he should bring Linda along in case she also wanted to take a crack at it.

So it was settled. On Sunday morning, in a gesture of chivalry, Marcelo insisted that Linda should go first. Stenio ran down the ramp and jumped off with Linda next to him. The ungainly device resembling a kite from which the two harnessed riders were hanging rose up to a considerable height. After a gentle curve to the left over the buildings that lined the coast, the glider veered down to the right towards a designated landing area on Sao Conrado beach. Suddenly something went terribly wrong. It made a loop in the opposite direction, winding down into a tailspin dive at great speed, and crashed to the pavement, killing both occupants instantaneously. Marcelo watched all this with an awful look of despair on his face, crying out loud: "Help! Oh, my God, they're both dead!"

He hopped into Stenio's jeep and drove back down to the beach. A feral look glinted in his eyes as he slumped over the wheel, clenching his teeth and muttering: "Now you can fuck your asses off in hell."

The police investigation resulted in nothing of merit to proceed with. In view of the great height of the fall and the force of impact, the hang glider was wrecked to pieces when it hit the ground, making it impossible to determine the cause of the accident.

A month later, Marcelo quit his job at the apartment building and moved out to Brasilia to take up the entrance exams and join the police force. That is how he became "Sweet Lip," the most polite, congenial and soft-spoken law-enforcement officer of the homicide division at the Thirty-Ninth Precinct in Brasilia.

Stereotypically being averse to violence and bloodshed, Marcelo was usually given the cases where there was suspicion of murder to find out the assassin's identity and whereabouts and inform his superiors, who would take legal action for the arrest.

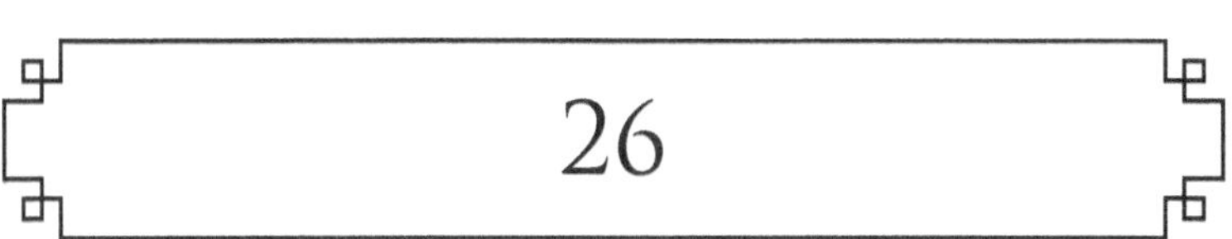

26

On the following afternoon, Hassan stopped by the gym and looked up Gamal.

"I can't see you tonight. I have work to do," he said. "The president is throwing a dinner party at the Palace for the President of Portugal. I've been assigned to the security detail."

Gamal was upset, but did not let it on.

"It's OK. We can talk tomorrow."

"Tomorrow's out, too. Guto's B-Day. I bought him a present."

Gamal was furious now. "What a crazy bastard!" he thought. "There he goes again, shirking off his life's intended mission because of a stupid kid's birthday party. The moron".

"All right!" Gamal said, concealing his strong feelings of displeasure. "And then what?"

"Then it'll be Saturday."

"What's wrong with Saturday?"

"Not a chance. That's when I pick up and clean out the house, mow the lawn, do my laundry, and wash and lube the bike."

Gamal was so furious that he could hardly control himself. "The idiot has not yet grasped the importance of my plan," he thought to himself. "I'm wasting my time with this jerk."

"What about my plan? You've said nothing about it."

"I'm still turning it over in my head. We'll talk about it come Monday, say, around sixish."

"I'm glad you haven't brushed off my ideas."

"Not at all. Yours is a serious notion, damned serious and… dangerous. I have to be focused, think the whole thing out. I'm taking the entire Sunday off just to give it careful consideration."

Gamal was turning the matter over and over in his mind. Experience told him that Hassan was going through a phase where he needed to overcome the fear that kept him from going ahead with the plan. So far this fear was greater than the will to carry out his vengeance."

"I see," Gamal said. "Ok! Then it's a date. Monday without fail." Gamal gave emphasis to the term "without fail."

"Agreed. See you Monday!"

Gamal watched as he walked out. All in all, the odds of bringing Hassan around to his way of thinking seemed favorable. He knew the recipe for success: skill, patience, persistence, and appeal to the good feelings of an emotionally frail Hassan were the essential ingredients for good results.

After teaching his last class and before going back to the hotel, Gamal dropped by the place where he kept the metal case which contained the components to assemble bombs gradually acquired from dealers through the cooperation of a prostitute who used the hotel for her tricks. Lit by his motorcycle's single headlight, he dug in the dirt a couple of feet and, without picking up the case, he opened up the lock, lifted the lid, pulled out a sheet of paper containing the list of the bomb's constituent elements, put it in his pocket, pushed the lock shut, filled the hole back up with dirt and headed for the hotel. Gamal wanted to make sure that he had enough TNT and C-4 on the list. Making a bomb from trinitrotoluene (TNT), a very sensitive and dangerous explosive, would not be the best idea. He felt inclined to use C-4, a plastic explosive that is extremely powerful yet stable and safe.

Upon arriving at the hotel, Gamal went straight to his room, climbed into bed, read and reread the list carefully. He virtually had all the essential components to assemble a few small bombs of great destructive power.

He fell asleep wondering what kind of explosive he could put together that would blow up the largest number of lives.

27

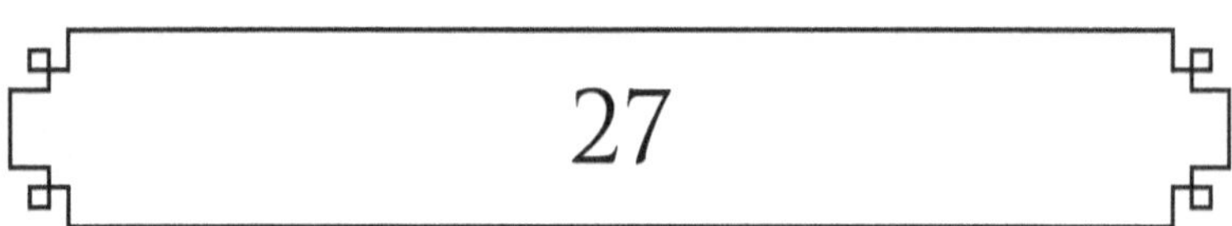

There were two motor lodges on the road nearby Iasci. Raquel and Mauricio had no luck in the first one where nobody knew the man in the picture. Farther off there was another one where they ran into a surprise.

"Oh yes! This man stayed here!" exclaimed the clerk at the front desk. "He was with two friends."

"Are you sure?" Mauricio asked out of sheer anxiety.

"Absolutely! The three paid cash in advance for a whole week. They took three adjoining rooms." He pointed to the picture. "This one was the only one who spoke Portuguese. They used a language among themselves that was totally unknown to me. It wasn't English or German, to be sure. I get around pretty well in English and I am of German descent. I even know a few expressions and phrases.

"How come you remember all the details?" Raquel asked.

"Not only because the situation was unusual, but the tip they gave me was lofty. That's not easy to forget."

"Were they speaking Arabic?" Mauricio wanted to know.

"Well, I don't know about that. I can't tell Arabic from Greek or Mandarin. Maybe it was. How would I know? It was a hell of a weird language, I'll tell you that. Really weird.

"And what did he say to you in Portuguese?

"He didn't want to be disturbed by anybody. They had all their meals in his room. That's why his room was between the other two with the interconnecting doors. I'll never forget that tip. Never got one nearly as close."

"And what else do you remember?" Raquel was beginning to get a little anxious herself.

The clerk brought his hand to his mouth in a gesture of recollection.

"OK," he said. "All three went straight to their rooms and stayed there throughout the week without so much as looking out the door. They spent their days together in the middle room. I'm not big on prying into the private affairs of others, but I confess I put my ear against the door a couple of times, although all I could hear was that strange lingo. On the weekend, the one who spoke Portuguese, that one,"— he pointed at the picture— "asked me to flag down a cab for him and left for Iasci. I never saw him again. Two days later, the other two checked out. They also vanished. Are you guys cops?"

"No!" Raquel was quick to reply. "We're with an insurance company."

The clerk, whose nickname was Fred, was relieved to hear that. No motel of that kind in Brazil is keen to have any sort of dealing with the police.

"Which would be our best bet to spend the night, Iasci or The Falls?" Raquel asked before she started up their rented car and began to pull out of the parking lot.

Before replying, Mauricio took his time to buckle up, crossed his arms and sat quietly looking out the windshield.

"Come to think of it, there's nothing going on in Iasci, whereas there's always a chance of something coming up, a coincidence, a chance encounter, in Iguazu Falls, which clearly seems to be their destination. Who knows?"

"Let's go back to The Falls then," said Raquel as she turned to get off on the exit.

In Iguazu Falls, they spent the night in an off-city-limits motel, which in Brazil is usually a short-stay hotel that affords couples privacy for sexual encounters as is also sometimes the case of motor lodges.

As predicted, there were no questions asked or, much less, ID cards and forms to be filled out.

Cuddled on the king-size round bed covered in mirrors with silhouettes of naked women painted on them, surrounded by tawdry scarlet walls, under indirect lighting and a mirrored ceiling, they managed to get some sleep after indulging and satisfying their lust for each other.

In the morning, inasmuch as nobody had seen the man in the photograph, they checked out and set off to make the rounds of the other motels in the outskirts of The Falls; but it was all to no avail. All the same, before making up their minds to head up to Brasilia, they decided to follow the circuit of the restaurants based Mauricio's recollection that his brother Eduardo at the luncheon with their parents in Braga, had mentioned the terrorist's desire to learn how to cook before coming over to Brazil.

"Perhaps he got a job as a chef's assistant somewhere?" he suggested.

"I think that's a far-fetched possibility," Raquel said. "As your brother himself said he wanted to *learn* how to cook. He can't have learned all that much in such a short time to land a job as chef's assistant," she inferred.

"Touché!" said Mauricio, acknowledging her effective point in argument. "But on the other hand nothing is keeping him from starting out as a bus boy or a dish washer. How many great cooks started from scratch just like that?"

"True enough," Raquel said, trying to conceal her feeling of doubt. "Let's start over. A thorough investigation should leave no gaps. No stone can be left unturned. Not even one."

They used the six following days to visit hotels and restaurants, showing the photograph and asking whether they had or had had anybody in the kitchen that resembled that man.

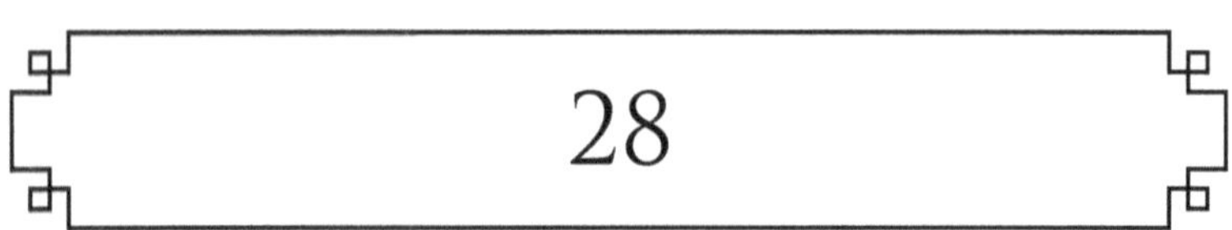

28

Thinking only of Jandira, Marcelo Moreira assigned a low priority to the investigation of watchman Jose Ignacio's death. The case became an excuse to see her when it suited him. He felt the first pangs of jealousy when she told him that she had once been engaged to be married, but due to an incompatibility of tempers they had broken off. The snag was that Jandira admitted that she was still in love with her ex-fiancé. "You understand, don't you?" she had asked Marcelo, who again was far from pleased when he learned that the Sergio, the dark man who had held her by the well, was madly in love with her. In fact, this combination of circumstances seemed to be foreordained by kismet. Marcelo was faced with an odd situation involving a beautiful woman and three men instead of the usual, eternal love triangle; but losing was never an option to him. He vowed to challenge the so-called power that predetermines events by doubling his efforts to win over Jandira's heart."

For the second time in his life he felt the urge to get married and have a family. He did not hold back because of doubt or uncertainty. He knew what he had to do. Therefore he decided that Jandira would be his wife.

Focused on always having a reason to meet up with her, he came up with all kinds of excuses related to the case. He had no scruple to resort to lies, if the end justified the means. Things however were not looking up. The ex-fiancé, Marcio, had run into Jandira downtown when they exchanged pleasantries and promised to discuss the possibility of making up.

And it got worse.

Sergio, the one with the comforting shoulder, went by the store every single day to chat with Jandira. On that very weekend, he invited her to a barbecue at his sister's home, and Jandira was quick and glad to accept. Marcelo had just stopped by to see Jandira at the exact moment that she was on her way out with Sergio and had no time for the detective.

As he stood there and watched the couple driving off in Sergio's old pickup truck, a disgruntled Marcelo could barely control his temper. His twisted mind was on fire and he could only think of vengeance. "If you think this ends here, that's all you know about it,"

he muttered, fists clenched shut and eyes refusing to believe such tribulation." He was hopelessly, insanely, frantically in love with Jandira.

29

On Monday, before five in the afternoon, Hassan, for the first time, arrived at the refuge and had to wait for Gamal.

"This is a first," the terrorist thought as he parked his motorcycle alongside of Hassan's. "Anyway, it sure is a good sign to see this unpredictable bastard here so early."

To Gamal's surprise, Hassan was in a good mood. He had had a great weekend, yet he whined about his loneliness and admitted to his eager anticipation to reunite with his beloved Raissa. Gamal took the opportunity to remark how lucky Hassan really was, because he would enter paradise after taking his revenge in a proper manner. He would be happy, content, and unblemished when he joined Raissa, thereby bringing great joy to Allah.

As he listened to Gamal's peroration, an emotional sigh trembled between Hassan's lips. Gamal delivered a panegyric of righteous vengeance, a vengeance to be soon carried out under optimistic odds, the consequences of which would dignify him and make him stand good in the eyes of Allah. Hassan did not see in his partner the element of inherent evil that emanated from Gamal's criminal character. He chalked up Gamal's behavior to the immense suffering caused by the loss of his siblings murdered by the Americans. Somehow, he felt there were a lot of things they had in common, in view of the unbearable pain that had brought them together in their similar misfortunes. Hassan could never find the sense to perceive the killer instinct that was a distinctive mark in Gamal's fanatical personality. He deemed the terrorist's reasoning for that sinister plan feasible and justifiable.

Hassan had not lost his straightforwardness, though.

"I've kept my promise," he said. "I thought about your plan the entire day yesterday. I believe it can be done if we do everything right. Let me in on how you intend to carry it out."

It took Gamal an immense effort to restrain himself from erupting in an outburst of joy and contentment when he heard this. He got up and did not even bother to brush the sand off his pants. He plunged his trembling hands in his pockets and turned his back on Hassan to hide the intense blush on his face brought on by the violent emotion of the moment. He stood there for a long while gazing at the ripple and the soft surf in the lake.

"What impresses me most about you is your penetrating mental discernment and clear-sightedness," Gamal finally said, trying to sound nonchalant.

Hassan was caught off guard. He wasn't expecting the compliment.

"That's kind of you," he said. "I'm just not dumb, is all."

By then Gamal had pulled himself together and again was sitting across from Hassan.

"I'm cool," he said. "Let's talk about this our plan, I mean, let's lay down the detailed steps of its execution."

Hassan had a question up front.

"You want to blow up a bomb. Why don't I just shoot him down and then blow my own brains out?

"I thought about that; but then again, looking back into every contingency, I realized it would be way too risky, because the shot may turn out not fatal, not to mention the possibility of a misfire. And suppose you miss! You'd be the only casualty, and then kiss your vengeance good-bye.

"Me? Miss a point-blank shot?"

"I think your missing a point-blank shot is not likely to happen, but it's not impossible, and, well, we just can't run any risks. Nothing can be left to chance. History is teeming with instances of unforeseen developments that saved the lives of people who were preordained to die. As you probably know, there were several unsuccessful attempts on Adolf Hitler's life. The last one, at Wolfsschanze on 20 July 1944, Colonel Stauffenberg entered a briefing room carrying a briefcase containing a small bomb and placed it under the conference table, as close as he could to Hitler. Some minutes later, he excused himself and left the room. After his exit, the briefcase was moved by Colonel Heinz Brandt. When the explosion tore through the hut, Stauffenberg was convinced that no one in the room could have survived. Although four people were killed and almost all survivors were injured, Hitler himself was shielded from the blast by the heavy, solid-oak conference table and was only slightly wounded. We can't let something like that happen to you."

"If I have a bomb strapped to my body, do you think nobody will notice it?"

"That's the beauty of it. Speaking from my vast experience handling explosives, I've learned to put together an artifact smaller than a hand grenade. As you know only too well, you can hold a 'pineapple' grenade in the palm of your hand. Whoever is within a radius of 16 feet when it goes off will be done for."

"Then I'll have to be less than 16 feet from the President of the United States?"

"I took that into account. I'm going to put in a timing device. When you set off the detonator, you'll have fifty seconds to position yourself. Try to be less than 16 feet from the infidel when the bomb explodes fifty seconds later. Fifty seconds is more than enough time for you to study and execute your move.

"How are you going to build a bomb so small, and yet so powerfully destructive?"

"Think of the size of a hand grenade. Then remember its power of destruction. The secret lies in the type of explosive to be used."

"But if I strapped a hand grenade to my body, the bulge would stand out."

"Like I said, it won't be like a grenade; it'll be something longer, but with less volume. Imagine a spectacles case just a mite larger than the usual spectacles case."

"I don't follow you."

"Don't you have an underarm rig for your gun?"

"Sure. That's where I keep the holster for my Colt.45."

"There you go! The bomb will replace your Colt. It'll take its place in the holster. It can only be seen if you open your jacket. I'll make a special holster for the bomb if it need be."

"We're not allowed to open our jackets when on duty."

"There you go! Even better! No need to fret about it."

"I'd like to pack a gun. Makes me feel safer. When you least expect… One never knows… I might need it.

"Is the Colt.45 the only handgun you've got?"

"No. I own other guns of smaller caliber."

"Any revolver?"

"A.38 short barrel."

"What about an ankle holster?"

"Good idea! Why didn't I think of that?"

Hassan wanted to know more.

"Can you really build a bomb that will fit into my Colt.45 holster?"

"Maybe a mite larger. We'll make a holster for the bomb. We still have twenty-four days until the ceremony on the flattop. I'll have plenty of time to build three practically identical bombs. We'll set one off as an experiment to make sure it works. You'll wear one and the third will be kept back as reserve. We need a place for our tryout. It'll have to be way off the beaten track where no one can hear it. This spot here is no good. It's too close to the freeway. Stands out like a sore thumb."

"We can talk about that later. How do I set off the device?"

"There'll be a cord connected to the detonator and attached to your belt. Jerk it sharply. I thought of rigging a remote control to trigger the explosion, but gave up. It's too complicated. From the instant you pull that cord, you'll have 50 seconds before the bomb blows up. It's time enough to get closer to the infidel. One thing, though. Don't forget this! Once you pull the cord and set off the detonator there'll be no turning back. The bomb will explode no matter what.

"You left nothing out, did you?"

"You better believe it. I can't miss out on the chance to help a friend carry out his vengeance. Ever since the notion popped into my head I haven't thought of anything else."

" "It'll take a lot of nerve to pull that cord without attracting any attention."

"We'll have to work on that. If it gets too tricky, I can always have it go through a belt loop and tie a hoop to it. You'll tug at the hoop."

Hassan was flabbergasted. Gamal had planned out the whole shebang down to the smallest detail.

"Can we pull this off," Hassan asked, "in spite of all that security apparatus?"

"You are an essential part of the apparatus, Hassan. Nobody will be checking out the president's most reliable bodyguard."

"The procedures are extremely thorough and efficient."

"I'm sure they are, but we have the edge on them this time around, don't we?"

"I guess…" Hassan muttered.

"I understand President Felipe and his bodyguards will arrive a few minutes before the ceremony begins. How long?"

"Fifteen minutes before. The Navy will fly them in on a chopper. He'll be escorted by six agents, including my boss, Colonel Blake. I'll be one of them. Then we'll wait for the other choppers that will ferry President Brian of the United States and all the presidents. We figure all this will take about half an hour until all of them take their seats at the huge table that will be placed outdoors on the flight deck. The security agents will line up behind the chairs of their respective presidents."

"Will anybody come near you guys?"

"Not near the agents, no. But there will be people coming and going with the papers, which are supposed to be signed."

"OK! Then let's plan our moves within that frame."

Hassan scratched his head, looking around for a moment, lost in his thoughts and wondering.

"I don't know," he said. "This sounds so freaking simple… Kind of scary, isn't it? Makes me have second thoughts whether it can really be done."

Gamal stood up, smiling.

"That's the secret formula that leads to success," he said. "Simplicity is the key to the achievement of things desired. Do you really believe that anybody would think that a very capable and highly-trusted security agent would gun down his own president? Why, man, you could've easily nailed the bastard any time. Why make a grandstand play of it?"

Hassan walked slowly towards his motorcycle followed by Gamal. They both mounted up.

"I like your plan," Hassan shouted, engine revving, "but we still have to exchange a few notes and notions."

"Tomorrow at fivish?" Gamal shouted back.

"Fine! See you then!"

Gamal let him drive off ahead. The terrorist felt a warm glow of satisfaction.

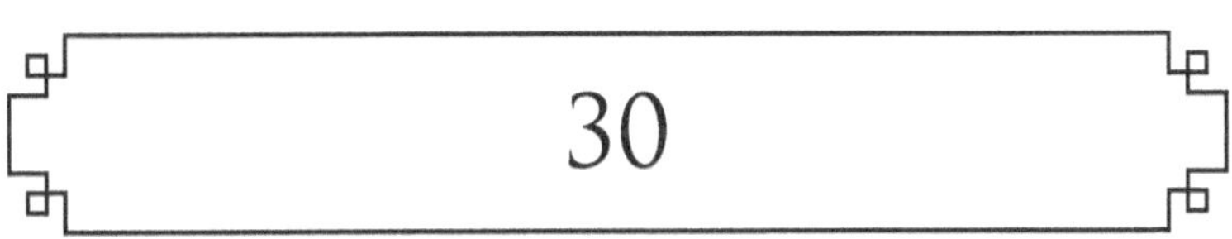# 30

As they wrapped up another bootless visit to a restaurant in Iguazu Falls, Raquel could not hide her disappointment.

"We're going to have to go back to Iasci, she said, sighing.

Mauricio was startled.

"Say what? Again?"

She looked in his face.

"We forgot to ask at the motel whether the clerk knew the cabbies that ferried the first terrorist and the other two afterwards."

"By golly, you're right! What are the odds?"

"Well, I wouldn't throw in my chips if the motel were here in The Falls; but Iasci is a whole new ballgame. Small town. Everybody is an acquaintance, if not a kin."

"Are we renting a car again?"

"Yep! We shouldn't have returned the other one."

"We did the right thing. Who'd imagine we'd be heading back? We really don't need a car here in The Falls. All kinds of transportation."

"Chief Cerveira is very concerned about keeping all this under wraps," Raquel said from behind the wheel. "Every e-mail from him is a reminder to keep an eye out for leaks."

"I noticed," said Mauricio. "I wonder why all this secrecy. Being discreet is one thing, but…"

"I believe it's because we're dealing with a terrorist here," she cut in. "It's a new experience for us. If this thing leaks to the press this whole operation is a goner."

Indeed, inasmuch as they were hunting a different kind of criminal, a man capable of mass slaughter who was prone not only to kill innocents but would not bat an eye dying in the process, Cerveira was quick to recommend the greatest care. Only after the terrorist was located, the police would be called out to make the arrest. Until such time, it would be up to the two agents to track him down. Cerveira feared that, since, on account of its novelties and Hollywood-like peculiarities, this case was big and would get a lot of media. It just might become easy for an agent, either unintentionally or in pursuit of fifteen minutes of fame, to leak it to a reporter. The news would spread quickly and the terrorist would slip through their fingers or, in the worst-case scenario, he would blow himself up taking God-knows-how-many lives with him. One way or the other, he would never be found.

It was evening when they pulled up in front of the motel.

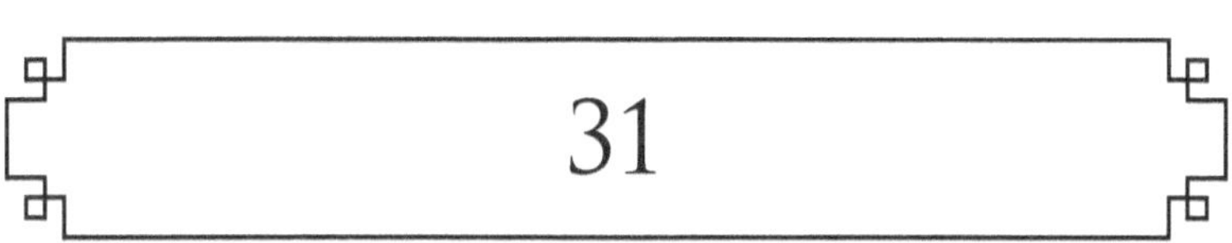

31

nxious to find any new angle in the watchman's murder investigation that would serve as an excuse to call on Jandira, Marcelo decided to scour the backyard of every house in that sector of the complex. He found a whistle, and, as he looked it over, he remembered a woman telling him how comforting it had been for her to hear, late at night, the blowing of Jose Ignacio's whistle out there. The detective went around the house to the front door and rang the doorbell. A woman came over to tell him that nobody lived there anymore.

"It used to be Sergeant Deivid's home. He died recently, poisoned by gas that leaked out of his bathroom. The cops said it was suicide."

He showed her the whistle, but she was not sure whether it belonged to the deceased watchman.

Back at his desk, again he gazed at the whistle, absorbed in his thoughts. "If this here whistle actually belonged to Jose Ignacio what the hell was it doing in the dead sergeant's backyard?"

Marcelo looked up the team that had worked on Deivid's case. He had a couple of questions to ask them. He learned that Luis and da Costa had assisted Chief Jose Lavradio, deputy director of internal investigations at Planalto Palace, the seat of federal government. Lavradio had ordered that their report should conclude that the sergeant's death had been the result of suicide.

"Say what? He *ordered* it?" Marcelo asked, dumbfounded. "And you took it lying down?"

"Of course I did!" Luis replied. "Da Costa refused to sign the damn report and they transferred his ass to Narcotics."

"I see… Well, was it *really* suicide?"

"No way! That dude was killed, to be sure. The high brass in the palace covered it up to dodge a scandal. Imagine the headlines: "DUMBASS PALACE EMPLOYEE WASTED. The media would have a field day."

"I'll go down to the palace to clear this up."

"Planalto?"

"Sure! Where else?"

"You watch your back, you hear? Want a piece of advice? Stay clear of Chief Lavradio. I was there when he came back with a direction straight from Olympus to end that investigation forthwith. He was fuming."

"I'll avoid him."

"It's the smart move."

Marcelo went home to change his clothes. Palace bureaucrats and guests had to wear jacket and tie.

As he was putting on his tie, wandering around the dining room, he noticed his small collection of small firearms left unattended on the table: two medium-frame.38 revolvers, a 9 mm pistol, the serial number of which had been scraped off, a silencer, a double-barrel muzzle-loading pistol, and a.22 revolver. They had been illegally procured from cutthroats, ruffians, and hoodlums in the course of police raids. He was in the habit of cleaning out his guns once a month and putting them away wrapped in flannel.

Marcelo donned his best suit. He pulled into the visitors' parking lot in the courtyard behind the palace. He walked into the garage, and, after flashing his badge, he addressed a group of men in overalls.

"I'd like to ask a few questions about Sergeant Deivid. I don't intend to see any of the big bosses. I just want to chat with his closest friends." They suggested he talk to Homero, who was due back from vacation next week. "He was the deceased's best friend."

He thanked them and drove off.

32

When they got together at the close of the afternoon, Hassan drew a sketch in the sand of the positions assigned to the security agents with respect to their presidents on the flight deck of the carrier *Rio de Janeiro*. President Felipe would occupy the central seat with Colonel Blake standing right behind him, Hassan on his left, and agent Homero on his right. Three more Brazilian agents would be lined up behind them: Jose Carlos, Celso, and Gustavo. Each president would have six bodyguards with a similar layout.

"Why will the American president sit to the left of President Felipe?" Gamal asked.

"The seating chart was set up according to the chronological order of adhesion to the agreement. The United States was the second country to sign in, shortly after Venezuela. President

Carlos Hernandez will be on our president's right-hand side. And so on, I mean, for the seats all along the table."

"As for you, over here," he pointed out a small mark on the sketch, "well, my friend, you'll be the Brazilian agent closest to the American president?"

"That's right. I enjoy the colonel's entire confidence."

"Indeed you are the chosen one," said Gamal without taking his eyes off the sketch. "The more I look at this here drawing, the more I am convinced that Allah picked you out to do His justice."

"It may well be true. It'll speed up my revenge."

Gamal still couldn't take his eyes off the sketch.

"Doesn't it strike you as peculiar that Colonel Blake, as head of Security and Intelligence, should play the role of a regular security agent?"

"No, not at all. It's been like this since our first briefing. When he took on this billet, he made it clear there was nothing in the regs that prevented him from acting like a plain, average agent. That's his way of stressing how important our job really is. To make his point he himself assumes the position of team leader in more relevant events. And he always stands right behind the president."

"Would you have a sketch of the layout of other officials and guests on deck and at the big table?"

"I do. I'll bring a copy to our next meeting. Can't let you have it, though."

"Nor do I want it. It's just that we need to have a broad, comprehensive view, but it's really not all that important."

Hassan wiped off the drawing with his feet.

"What about the bomb?" he asked

"I'm sorting out the ingredients."

"Do you need any money?"

"If I had to buy weapons, yes, but I have the basic, the indispensable components to put together two or three small bombs. Whatever is missing, I will pay the trafficker with my life savings. He'll deliver the goods tomorrow," he lied.

Gamal already had everything.

"If you need money, I can chip in."

"Don't worry about it. It's not much. Thanks, anyway."

Fanaticism puts blinders on people. Hassan had always been a fanatic, but never knew it. Obsessed with the idea of revenge and meeting up with his bride in the afterworld, he never realized the extent of Gamal's overstatements, lies, fabrications, and contradictions; worse yet, manipulations.

Hassan looked at his watch.

"Today's Tuesday," he said. "Tomorrow I'm going to Cuba and Honduras with the president. We'll be back Friday night. What say we meet here Saturday morning?"

"Super!" exclaimed Gamal. "I'll have the three bombs ready by then. The simplest one will be our tryout. We'll set it off and see how much damage it can cause. We've got to find an out-of-the-way site for that. The other one will be your baby to carry; it'll be the most elaborate and also the most powerful. The third one will be kept on standby."

"We can meet right here on Saturday morning," said Hassan, "and head out towards Goiania. We'll drive along for half an hour and then swerve off the road into the woods. We can run our test way out in the sticks. How does it sound?"

"Sounds perfect," said Gamal.

"Alright then. Let's mosey!" said Hassan.

Gamal headed straight for the shopping mall in Brasilia. At a stationery store he bought pencils, erasers, a notepad, a ball of string, duct tape and a plastic wire reel. In a small bazaar he purchased three high-quality small alarm clocks. Afterwards he went to the gym and taught his night classes.

On the way back to his hotel, at one point, he veered out into the woods and followed a long-abandoned trail. Again, with the aid of the motorcycle's headlights, Gamal unearthed the metal case. He used a length of the string to fasten it to his bike, covered up the hole and made the way back up the trail.

In his room, he put the case in the closet. He sat down at the dresser, pulled out the pencil and notebook, and made a list of all the items needed to build a bomb. He got the case from the closet, took out the components to be used, and placed them in a shoebox. Gamal put everything away, took a shower, and donned clean underwear and a T-shirt. He went to the refrigerator, made a cheese sandwich, and drank some water. He had classes in the morning, so the bombs would have to be built in the afternoon. By the time Hassan got back, they would be ready to go.

33

Raquel and Mauricio did not find Fred, the clerk. It was his day off, but he would be back in the morning; so they thought it best to spend the night there in the motel. Like all motels in Brazil, this one was a "love hotel," that is, the type of short-stay joint operated primarily for the purpose of allowing couples privacy to have sexual intercourse. The room was decorated in extraordinary poor taste. However, the delicious dinner they had been served was highly commendable.

After reading the e-mail from chief Cerveira and discussing it with her partner, Raquel was plagued by a splitting migraine. She lay down and finally managed to fall asleep. Lying by her side, Mauricio found himself enveloped in a swirl of memories. He sat up in bed and reviewed the latest developments. A throb of strong uneasiness caused by an unbearable sense of loss stung him when he thought about going back to Lisbon and leaving

Raquel behind. Watching her in her sleep, he was overrun with a profound sense of tenderness immediately followed by a great sorrow; a sorrow so great that he could not prevent the tears from rolling down his cheeks and dissolving between his lips. Mauricio reached for his handkerchief and dried his eyes, but more tears welled up to replace the ones he had wiped away. He sat there in the dark, crying softly. If asked why he was shedding so many tears, he would not know what to say. However, deep inside, where the most intense affective state of consciousness, such as that resulting from emotions, sentiments, or desires are engendered, an anguished pain mingled with a strong dose of anxiety emerged as a prelude to the loneliness that would be installed in his soul when the time came to say good-bye. He dreaded that day, because he knew what it felt like. He had been down that road before. A previous experience had taught him a dire lesson. Solitude would cast its long shadow over him as it did when his fiancée, the lovely Fatima, on the eve of their wedding, left him in the lurch and made up with an ex-boyfriend who was now her husband. Mauricio got out of bed, went to the balcony, and looked out into the night. The sky was a canopy of stars. As the churchgoing Catholic that he was, Mauricio prayed: "Heavenly Father, help me! I've already suffered way too much because of a broken heart. Don't let it happen again!" He went back to bed alongside of Raquel ever so quietly. Suddenly an aphorism coined by Antoine de Saint-Exupery came to mind: *"You risk tears if you let yourself be captivated."* "What about when you let yourself fall in love?" he thought before falling asleep.

The two got up shortly after seven. Raquel was all smiles, since the headache was gone. They had breakfast in their room and went to talk to Fred.

"Of course I remember who the driver was. He's one of our regular cabbies that drive our guests back and forth: Mr. 'Big Head' Antonio. There are four cars at the taxi stand and two drivers by the name of Antonio. Well, to avoid confusion, since one of them is endowed with a big head, they dubbed him 'Big Head' Antonio and… well, he was the driver who picked up the fellow who spoke Portuguese and gave me a great tip. We always call the same drivers, because…"

"All right, you made your point!" Raquel broke in. "I'm sorry, but we're in a big hurry here. Where can we find Mr. Big Head, I mean, this Mr. Antonio."

"There's only one taxi stand in town. It's on Main Street. You can't miss it. He can come up here if you flag him down. Want me to call him up?"

"What about the other two that checked out on the next morning or two days later?" asked Mauricio.

"The same Antonio," Fred chuckled.

"No need to call him, we'll drive down to the stand," said Raquel, handing out her credit card for the checkout.

At the taxi stand they were told that Big Head had taken a couple of tourists to Iguazu Falls. He would be back late that night, so they could only see him the next morning around seven. They parked the rented car near the stand and went arm in arm for a walk on the town. One hour later they passed in front of the small factory of stringed instruments. Mauricio considered buying the guitar in the showcase, but discarded the idea, inasmuch as it would be rather uncomfortable to travel with such a bulky extra piece of luggage.

It was near 11 o'clock when they sat down for a drink on a restaurant terrace. They were dismayed as they reviewed the progress of their investigation to date: it virtually amounted to nothing. If they had not been tipped off about the terrorist's trip to Brasilia, they would be starting over from scratch. They made the decision to follow their quarry to the federal capital after their talk with Mr. Big Head. The snag was that they would arrive in Brasilia without a single clue as to Gamal's whereabouts. Finding a cook would be a shot in the dark. The police could hardly help them, since there had been no feedback from them with regard to the notice issued by chief Cerveira.

They left the restaurant and drove out to Iguazu Falls for lunch. In the evening, just to be on the safe side, they went back to Iasci and checked into the hotel nearest to the taxi stand where, early in the following morning, Mr. Big Head Antonio was waiting for them.

34

Encouraged by the consistent improvement of his relations with Jandira, Marcelo was happy when she agreed to go steady with him. They started to meet at night, three times a week, Wednesdays, Saturdays, and Sundays at her place. She had to work on the other days of the week to supplement her salary, laboring over her sewing, mending clothes for her customers.

On Monday he dropped by the garage and learned from Homero that Deivid was a good pal, albeit a little bashful. "He was striving to become one of the president's bodyguards. He was even attending a gym to improve on his self-defense abilities," Homero told him, "and target-practicing over at his former brother-in-law's ranch, a fellow by the name of Alceu who was manager at Monte Branco Mart located on the third North Wing superblock."

Marcelo took new heart and decided to have a chat with Alceu and pay a visit to the gym.

He saw Alceu on that same afternoon. He learned something about Deivid's life. "His wife left him," said Alceu who disapproved of his sister's attitude. "Deivid was a fine man, even-tempered and good-natured. He led a quiet life. Drank very seldom. Didn't smoke. As of late, as far as I know, all he did was perfect his marksmanship out on my ranch."

As for the gym, Alceu didn't say much. "It's over on the North Wing… Olympic Academy of Martial Arts, I think it's called".

Marcelo was satisfied with all the information he had obtained in one day's work. He had plenty of excuses to swing by Jandira's place and let her in on everything he had dug up; even if it violated the visiting schedule they had agreed upon. It was Monday. He just could not wait until Wednesday.

He stopped by the precinct, sat at his desk, took a few notes, and headed for Jandira's apartment.

It was 8:30 p.m. when he parked across from his girlfriend's building. He saw Jandira go in arm in arm with a man he had never seen before.

Mad with jealousy, all of a sudden he felt his breath come fast and ragged from the charge of adrenaline pulsing through his veins. Marcelo started to get out of the car to check things out, but thought better of it. He settled back into the seat and mused carefully and slowly about his options. "Who the hell was that?" he asked himself. "Easy does it! Better wait it out!"

He just sat there and waited for time to pass. At 2:30 in the morning, he was desperate. "The son of a bitch was spending the night with her." Marcelo turned on the ignition and geared up to call it a day and go home. He sped along the freeway, filled with hatred toward Jandira. "That bitch doesn't know who she's messing with," he grumbled.

Before turning in, he tried to devise a plan for revenge. "It's got to be perfect… just like the one I cooked up for that son of a bitch Stenio and that whore Lindalva."

By the time he fell asleep, around five o'clock in the morning, Marcelo had everything schemed out, so that, in his sick mind, it appeared impossible for him to fail.

35

Having in hand the necessary components he needed to build all the three bombs, Gamal began working on the first one on Sunday after lunch. He started out by dismantling one of the hand grenades he had in the metal case. He deactivated the fuse mechanism and pulled out the percussion cap, splitting the grenade open in halves. Then he removed the metal balls fused to form the shrapnel that would fan out in all directions with the explosion.

By evening it was ready. Since he had no holster— Hassan was wearing his own— Gamal improvised one as a makeshift. He cut out a plastic sheet according to the dimensions of a leather case shaped to hold a.45 pistol just to have an idea of volume. He placed the bomb under his right arm strapped to the plastic sheet with strings and duct tape. When he put on his jacket, he noticed it was too bulky. "Too much shrapnel," he thought. "I'll build a smaller one tomorrow afternoon."

He was quite satisfied. The clock struck ten. He gobbled up a sandwich, took a shower, and lay down in bed on his back, with ankles crossed and fingers interlaced behind his head like a pillow. Staring up at the ceiling, he plunged into memories in retrospect of events since his arrival in Brazil: the days spent in Sao Paulo, the trip to Iguazu Falls, the conference at Iasci with two companions on their way to Buenos Aires, who like him stood by for instructions from headquarters. He went through the two-day discussions in the motel and, after leaving his cronies, his meeting with Soraya, an operative posted in The Falls. She had instructed him that, in the event of a crisis, he should make contact through snail mail. Under no circumstances was he to communicate directly with the cell leadership. So far he had never felt the need to get in touch with his superiors. He considered his choice to operate out of Brasilia a gift from heaven. "That's where I can do the most good," he mused, "with all the big shots and foreign dignitaries." Of course, when headquarters learned that he, Gamal Abdul, had been responsible for Hassan's magnificent accomplishment, taking out several leaders of western democracies, including the President of the United States, he would be blessed and glorified; even perhaps he, Gamal Abdul, would move on up to the high command of al Qaeda.

In truth, he preferred to continue as a suicide bomber. His mind was warped by the indoctrination lavished upon him in an al Qaeda boot camp. He was totally imbued with a partisan, ideological view of a fanatically religious nature, as a result of a life-or-death brainwashing against all western values. Gamal was absolutely convinced that, by sacrificing his own life and wiping out a large number of infidels, he would please

Allah and be deserving of the supreme reward of living in a paradise surrounded by gorgeous virgins, enjoying luxury and wealth, in the loveliest of places, unimaginable by any ordinary human being.

With a bomb on the dresser and a metal box in the closet containing four grenades, three dynamite sticks, a few tools, six chunks of the potent C-4 explosive, two 9 mm pistols, plenty of ammunition, and a package of gunpowder, Gamal slept quietly, happily, with a contented expression on his face.

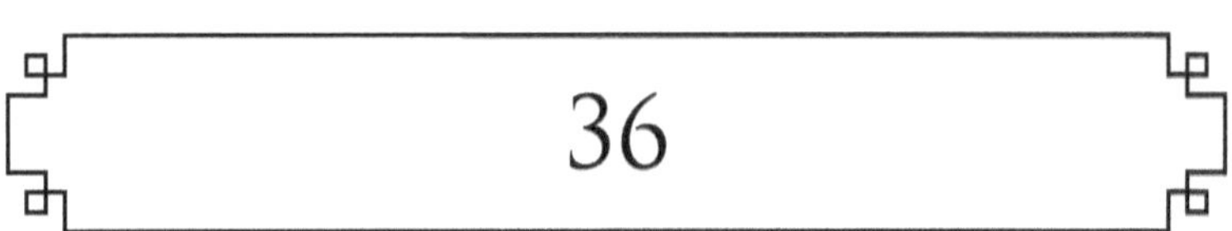

36

In the course of their talk with the cabby named Antonio Big Head, Raquel and Mauricio were surprised by the input that there was someone else linked to the terrorist: a woman.

"This man," the cabby said pointing to Gamal's picture, "asked me to take him to Rua Ferreira Prado, a street not far from here. There was a woman waiting for him on the sidewalk.

"Did you take a good look at her?" Raquel asked.

"She was dark. They shook hands and, I think, walked into the building in front of which I'd stopped to drop him off. Can't be sure of that, though."

The detectives did not expect anything like that, but they did their best to keep their poise.

"Please take us there," said Mauricio.

Big Head pulled over in front of a five-story building.

"This is it," he said. I think they went in there," he pointed.

"What about the other two?" Mauricio asked. "You picked them up the next day, didn't you?"

"Sure did. Drove them straight down to the interstate bus station."

"Where were they headed?"

"I haven't the foggiest idea. I dropped them off and drove away."

"Even so, you have a sharp memory," Raquel remarked.

"They gave me a fat tip. You never forget a passenger that overtips you. To tell the truth, I'd never been given a good tip before them in all these years."

Raquel paid the cabby and gave him a good tip, too. He smiled his gratitude at her, and she nodded. He drove off, and the two detectives stood in front of the building.

"Do you suppose there is a terrorist network right here?" Mauricio asked, frowning.

"It there is, we're in a hell of a tight, dangerous spot here. This is a very serious situation. Way too serious," Raquel replied in a soft tone of voice.

For nearly half an hour they moved about without purpose near the building.

"This new info sure is disconcerting," Raquel broke the silence. "I suppose we should go back to the same hotel we stayed in last night. I'll send an e-mail with a situation report to Chief Cerveira and we'll wait here for his instructions. We'll have to put off our trip to Brasilia for a couple of days."

"You're right," said Mauricio. "This woman popped out of nowhere and messed things up."

"Something needs to be done," she said. "A terrorist network in Brazil is preposterous."

The walked all the way back to the hotel, checked in again and went straight up to their room.

In a long, detailed e-mail message to Cerveira, Raquel wrote out a full report to bring her boss up to date with the latest developments.

She closed her message with: "We are standing by for your instructions."

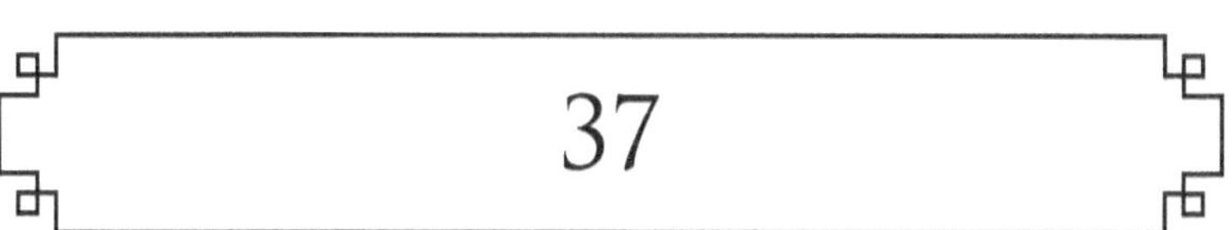

37

Marcelo woke up early. He was in a hurry to go back to his desk at the precinct and wrap up the update of his investigation report on Jose Ignacio's murder. He did that on a daily basis, adding on the latest inputs. As he leafed through his draft, he noted that progress was too slow. Anyway, inasmuch as he was dealing with the death of an underling, his boss, Chief Rubens, would not be breathing down his neck. "Had the victim been a rich man or a big shot," he thought, "old man Rube would be on my case like a fly on shit."

He had caught his girlfriend gallivanting with another man and could think of nothing except revenge. Under the pretext of checking out the veracity of the latest information, he spent the day roaming around the housing complex. At night he parked near Jandira's place and staked her out. He wanted to be absolutely certain that she was cheating on him. On

Thursday and Friday there were no callers, except for three women, possibly customers. On Saturday his girlfriend invited him to lunch at her home. He was not happy to see Sergio there. It was his birthday, so the lunch was for him, not for Marcelo. Struggling to control his anger, Marcelo managed to make polite conversation. Sergio proved to be friendly and good-natured. He gave Marcelo his business card and offered his services as an insurance salesman. After lunch, Sergio thanked Jandira and took his leave.

Marcelo and Jandira spent the weekend together, but he continued the stakeout on Monday and Tuesday nights. On Thursday, around 9:00 p.m., his suspicions were confirmed. Jandira and the stranger walked together arm in arm into the house. Just as he had planned, Marcelo sat in his car until 2:00 a.m. Only then he pulled on a pair of latex gloves, snapping them as he did. He walked around the house to the back door which he easily unlocked with a small, sharp-pointed instrument used for making eyelet holes in needlework that he had stolen from Jandira. He tiptoed through the house with the aid of a flashlight and moved stealthily into the bedroom where on a rather large bed two figures slept with their backs turned to one another. He drew his pistol with a silencer attached. The first well-aimed shot was fired at the stranger's head; the second bullet went straight in between Jandira's eyes. Soon their mixed bloods gushed out all over the bed sheets and floor. "That's what I call a quick, efficient job," he muttered.

Marcelo made the way back out of the bedroom towards the front door. He unlocked it, and left it ajar. Then he returned to the kitchen, sneaked out the back door, got into his car and went home.

He stayed up all night. At about half past nine, he read Sergio's business card and headed for the address on it. He saw the old pickup parked in front of a line of stores and pulled into a space four places ahead. He put on the latex gloves and walked towards Sergio's pickup. The doors were conveniently unlocked. He placed the pistol and silencer under the driver's seat, closed the door quietly, and sidled up back to his car. He never saw the "flannel boy" devouring a sandwich, sitting on a bench across the parking lot. Flannel boys are a plague typical of Brazil. They are illegal, extortionist, curbside parking attendants who have taken over the streets to brazenly and persistently importune drivers. They act like car jockeys, jumping in front of the car at traffic lights and stop signs, like the squeegee men eliminated from New York by Mayor Giuliani, wiping the windshield with a dirty flannel rag, and refusing to budge until tipped. They have also appropriated all the parking spaces in town and offer to watch cars for a not always small tip; when refused they slash tires, break taillights, put gravel in the gas tank, disconnect the carburetor, and so forth.

Marcelo arrived back at the precinct at ten-forty. He talked with some colleagues, pretended to take notes, and said he was going over to the gym for an interview with friends of the late Deivid's.

He pulled up in front of the gym next to a motorcycle and a man about to climb on it.

"Nice bike," he said to the man.

"Thanks. Kind of old, though. Been on the road five years."

Marcelo smiled and headed for the reception desk. There he was told that Deivid had indeed frequented the gym for wrestling classes three times a week with personal trainer Abdul.

"Coach Abdul has just left the building," said the receptionist. "He'll be back tonight around seven. He teaches mornings and evenings. Why don't you come back later?"

"You're sure he's not still around?" he said looking at his watch. "It's barely a couple of minutes past noon. Do you know where he lives?"

"He's gone. I heard the roar of his bike when he took off. He lives at the Bajara Hotel."

"Oh! The fellow on the motorcycle?"

"That's right. Looked Arabian, did he?"

"That's him all right. He lives at the Bajara, you say? I know where it is. I'll be back tonight."

He went back to the precinct.

Meanwhile, at the store where Jandira used to work, her employer and good friend Norma found it strange that she had not yet come in; it was late, and to make things worse today was inventory day. She got restless and decided to take her lunch break to drop by Jandira's home just a few blocks down the street. She rang the doorbell, but there was no answer. The door was ajar. She entered.

"Hello! Anybody home?" she hollered.

She went through the silent dining room and stopped at the hallway.

"Jandira, it's me, Norma. Are you in there?"

Still no answer.

The bedroom door was also ajar. Norma pushed it open and let out a scream at the bloody sight before her eyes.

"Whoa! Holy Virgin Mary! That's horrible!"

Shivering from head to toe, she ran out of the house, dialed the emergency number on her cellphone and shouted into it: "Police! Police! Help! A horrible thing!"

Half an hour later, three squad cars pulled up with sirens blasting, scaring neighbors and bystanders. One of the cars had brought detective Marcelo Moreira, of the homicide division, who had been assigned the case.

As the bodies were carried out of the house on stretchers to the morgue van, the detective wanted to have a word with Norma.

"Excuse me, ma'am. I'm detective Moreira. Please tell me everything you know about this."

A tremulous, sobbing Norma recounted the events from the moment she had noticed that her dear friend was not in the store.

"Why did you come here?"

"Because today we were going to go over the inventory, and Jandira always takes care of that."

Frowning, Marcelo made several notes in a notebook. He had thoroughly examined the bedroom and surroundings for clues and directed the police photographer to take some specific pictures. He did not want anybody moving anything. The police collected forensic evidence, sealed off the house, and left a trooper to stand guard and keep out the curious.

Back at the precinct, he went to see the chief.

"This crime may be related to the one I'm investigating. The woman was the daughter of the watchman whose body we found in that well near the military housing complex."

"Did you know her?"

"I did, sir. We talked on three occasions after her father's body was found. She was grateful for my efforts and even invited me to a lunch last Saturday to celebrate one of her friend's birthday. My investigation brought a few interesting facts to my attention. They may turn out to be a great help to get to the murderer."

"For example?" asked detective Luiz, who was also in Chief Rubens's office.

"Let's not put the cart before the horses," said Marcelo. "It's still early to assert anything. I intend to clear up a lot of doubts soon enough."

"Go for it!" said the chief. "The sooner we wrap up this case the better. We're dealing with a double murder with a good chance of being connected to another one: the murder of one of the victim's father. This is serious business. I want you to devote yourself entirely to this investigation, my boy."

Marcelo drove back to the housing complex where he moved about without purpose or plan, asking pointless questions with the sole purpose of gaining time and framing Sergio.

In the evening he showed up at the gym, looked up coach Gamal Abdul, and asked about sergeant Deivid.

"His presence here at the gym lasted only a short time," Gamal told him. "We had three classes, and he vanished. I'm waiting for him to return. I've managed to arrange a suitable schedule for him. Why do you ask?"

"He'll return no more!" Marcelo declared gravely. "He committed suicide."

"He what?" Gamal was visibly shocked.

"He was found dead in his bedroom from gas poisoning."

"Well I'm dashed!" Gamal exclaimed. "What can I do to help?"

"I'm trying to figure out why that young man committed suicide."

"We never noticed anything strange about him. Perhaps he was down in the

dumps for some reason, a woman maybe…"

"I'll take that under advisement."

"You see, officer, we only had three sessions, surely not enough to learn anything about a trainee."

"Yeah, I understand. Thanks, anyway."

Marcelo gave his card to Gamal before he left, asking the Arab to let him know should he come across any new information. Gamal's only concern was the execution of his plan— the event on the carrier was only a couple of weeks away— so he felt relieved after Marcelo was gone.

At noon the next day Marcelo turned in a brief report in which he suggested that, through a court order, a detailed inspection should be made at the home, office, and pickup of Mr. Sergio Gomez, suspected of murdering Jandira da Silva and Marcio de Oliveira. The motive was insane jealousy. In the course of the investigation it had been ascertained that the suspect visited Jandira da Silva every day at lunch time and that he was madly in love with the victim.

The report went on to state that, possibly, upon discovering the affair between Marcio de Oliveira and Jandira da Silva, he killed the couple when he found them in bed together after breaking into the house in the middle of the night. Inasmuch as no murder weapon had been found, a stringent search of the suspect's belongings was called for to justify an indictment.

On Thursday afternoon, insurance broker Sergio Gomes had his home and his office raided by the police. Brandishing a warrant, they turned everything inside out. When they went to his truck, they found a 9 mm pistol, a silencer, and two spent cartridges under the driver's seat. To make matters worse, the serial number had been scraped off. There were no fingerprints.

Sergio was handcuffed, despite his protests and taken to a common, filthy cell, because he had never graduated from college. In Brazil they found a way to class discrimination through law. Prison conditions are sub-human, but, strange as it may sound, if the criminal has a college degree he will not be put in the same cell with the rabble. That was not Sergio's case and he was charged with double first-degree murder pleads.

38

Gamal used up the afternoons throughout the week to make bombs. All three were ready on Friday. He built one large, one medium, and one small.

After several attempts to adjust each one to the makeshift plastic holster attached by straps under his left arm, he put on his jacket and saw that the medium-size one fitted best. He needed some sort of holster to fit it properly, though. Since Hassan would only be back at the end of next week, he concentrated on the finishing details.

As soon as Hassan got back Saturday morning, they would set off the smaller bomb and evaluate its power of destruction. They still had a whole week after that for the final arrangements. Early in the morning of next Friday, the Brazilian president and his entourage would be traveling back East to Rio de Janeiro. There, from the air base, a helicopter would ferry them straight to the aircraft carrier's flight deck.

That Sunday, by dint of a hefty tip, Gamal talked Katya, the whore who was his contact with the traffickers, into taking him on the afternoon of the next day to a cobbler or any other craftsman in the favela who worked with leather. He wanted to order a different kind of holster for a special weapon. In favelas one can find carpenters, masons, plumbers, painters, artists, and a large variety of other skilled, self-employed laborers. It did not take long for them to get to a manufacturer of designer Louis Vuitton imitation handbags, fake Prada design purses, and other famous brands of leather accessories who would be willing to make a special rectangular leather holster according to Gamal's specifications. It was very easy for Nelson, an expert forgery artist, at the heart of the Bat Cave Favela, to mold and sew Gamal's order to perfection.

Once he chose the medium-size bomb the one to be carried by Hassan, the terrorist did his best to make it as close to perfection as possible. He did so by adding very fine needles to the shrapnel-producing parts that he had extracted from one of the grenades thereby increasing its power of destruction. As an experiment, he did the same to the smaller bomb to see how it turned out. On Friday, it was all done. Gamal was looking forward to the return of his partner.

Saturday morning, Gamal arrived early at the refuge. Hassan was already waiting for him. They talked and exchanged ideas. Hassan apologized for not having the sketch. He had completely forgotten about it. After examining the bomb, he said nothing. They climbed on their motorcycles and took the interstate towards the city of Goiania. Forty minutes later they got off on an exit that led to a vicinal gravel road. The savanna is mostly grasslands with some bushes and trees. They left the gravel road after ten minutes and plunged into the wilderness through a field way off the beaten track, until they reached a clearing at the edge of a dense thicket. Gamal picked a flat area that seemed to be the closest they would get to something that somewhat resembled the flight deck of the aircraft carrier. He placed the try-out bomb on a small sand knoll; then he took six empty oil cans they had brought in their backpacks, filled them with sand and laid them out 15 feet from the knoll. They turned away and shielded themselves behind a tree. Gamal pulled a nylon thread attached to the detonator. The bomb went off. The cans were thrown a great distance. The knoll vanished. The terrorist could not contain his joy.

"Great! Excellent!" he almost shouted.

"I liked it, too," said Hassan.

"You realize that one end of a nylon thread just like this one will be fastened to the detonator on your bomb. The other end will go under your belt attached to a metal ring. At the right moment you'll pull on it hard. Now, as I've already told you, that will set off the process and the bomb will go off in fifty seconds," Gamal explained after he looked over the site of the explosion.

"What if it doesn't?" asked Hassan.

"That will never happen. Just pull it hard. No sound will be heard when you pull it so as not to attract attention. It *will* explode, believe you me. I've run this routine about ten times already."

"You really know the ropes," Hassan said with a smile.

"Those ten years I worked at the explosive factory are beginning to pay off."

"I'd like to see the bomb I'll be carrying."

"Next time we meet at the refuge, which will be this coming Monday, wear your full bodyguard outfit; jacket, tie, the works. We'll try on the holster with the straps… and the real bomb."

"No can do," Said Hassan. "I'm going to see Guto. I 've brought him a present."

Gamal had gotten used to that sort of attitude from Hassan. He thought to himself: "Here we are, talking about something of the utmost importance and this wacko is worried about some stupid brat. Now I know for sure it's not brownnosing. He must really love that kid."

"I understand," Gamal said in a condescending tone. How about Tuesday?"

"No problem," Hassan replied. "Let's make it Tuesday at 5 p.m. I'll go from the palace straight to the refuge."

"It's a date," said Gamal. "Remember: we only have Tuesday, Wednesday, and Thursday. You'll be off to Rio on Friday. It's the big day."

"I'm well aware of that," Hassan said. "The explosion was very powerful. Did you notice that it blew the leaves off the trees twenty yards away?"

"Sure did," Gamal chuckled. "I like that very much… but the bomb attached to your body will do a lot more damage."

They were both content on the way back to Brasilia.

39

The e-mail from Raquel did not surprise Cerveira. He already suspected that the turmoil in the area of the Brazil-Paraguay border near that bridge had a reason: a considerable amount of stolen cars, drugs, smuggled goods of all kinds, including arms, thus giving rise to an problem that was virtually impossible to solve, in light of the meager presence of police personnel. They had to struggle with the enormous task of enforcing law and order, so it was nearly impossible to divert their attention to odd kinds of activities such as potential acts of terrorism. Cerveira printed out the e-mail from Raquel and pulled up more information on his computer. Among the pertinent facts that he managed to dig up was a request from the United States Central Intelligence Agency (CIA) for an investigation by the Brazilian Federal Police regarding the likely activities of the Moroccan Islamic Combatant Group (*GICM* in the French initialism). The quiet, covert, detailed inquiry and systematic examination so far carried out by the Feds produced records that revealed Islamic fighters with cells in Morocco and Europe. They wanted to expand by taking their deadly business across the Atlantic Ocean to South America; more specifically, to South America's regional center for illegal activities, the Triple Frontier, where they intended to deploy their main base of operations. However, they had not yet found anything relating to an actual, particular incident or instance that they could put their finger on.

The input received from Raquel and Mauricio reinforced the probability of a potential presence of terrorists in Brazilian territory besides the suspect they were after.

Cerveira directed Raquel and Mauricio to proceed to Brasilia, after a thorough survey of the area upon which they had placed the most suspicion. They were to ascertain the existence of any trace of the woman linking her to the terrorist who had ridden in that taxi and then forward him a brief report. They should refrain from seeking the cooperation of the local Federal Police, because they were swamped and short of labor.

The coupled roamed around Iguazu Falls and adjacent towns for a few days. They interviewed the janitor at the building where the driver said he had seen the woman enter with the terrorist.

"No, ma'am," the janitor said. "I've had this job ever since they put up this building.

All residents have lived here for a long time. Actually, it's one big family. They're all

kinfolk, related somehow."

"What about the building next door?" asked Mauricio.

"Oh, I wouldn't know anything about it. A lot of people live there. Ring up the doorman's bell over there. His name is Manuel, a good man."

They learned from Manuel that Soraya had rented a flat on the fifth floor for a year. Habitually untalkative, she never greeted anybody and seldom left the apartment. She had no telephone line and used only a prepaid cellphone. Then one day she simply up and left; paid off all her bills and moved out. She never got any mail, either.

"She's the one!" exclaimed Raquel.

"She *was* the one," Mauricio emended. "She's probably a long way from here by now. Do you know where she was headed?"

"No, I don't! When I asked her she told me she was headed for a lot of places, but wasn't coming back to Iguazu Falls to be sure."

They went back to the hotel where they spent the day drafting up a report for consideration by chief Cerveira.

On the next day they crossed over the bridge into Paraguay, visited a few stores in Ciudad del Este, and returned to Iguazu Falls. After a last night in the hotel they traveled to Brasilia.

They reached the capital of Brazil on Tuesday afternoon. Their plane touched down at the very same moment when Ibrahim Hassan tried on the holster made especially for the bomb under his arm, buttoned up his jacket and heard Gamal say to him:

"It's perfect. Congratulations!"

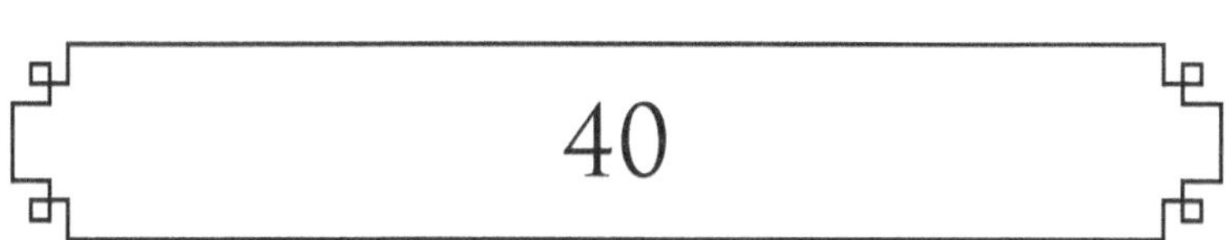

40

A photograph of detective Marcelo Moreira, the man in charge of the investigation, was on page four of the newspaper's police news section. It featured an extensive article on the murder of Marcio and Jandira in their sleep. Officer Homero showed it to Police Chief Jose Lavradio.

"This detective, Marcelo Moreira, was here the other day, asking questions about the late sergeant Deivid."

Lavradio immediately took the paper to his boss, Commissioner Romualdo Sodre.

"Get in touch with the Homicide Division and send for this detective," Sodre ordered. "The inquiry concerning sergeant Deivid's death is closed. This administration is better off if they don't try to reopen it. I'll put an end to this, and I'll do it my way."

Lavradio had a hunch what was coming next. Marcelo Moreira would be transferred out to another department, because he was a nuisance. He called Chief Rubens and told him he would like to see detective Moreira in his office at noon the next day.

"It's off the record," he said. "All I want is to show him the final report on Sergeant Deivid's suicide."

"Don't worry about it. I have a copy of that report," Rubens replied.

"I know. I want to personally explain to him why my signature is on that piece of paper. I was present when Da Costa and Luiz examined that bathroom gas wall heater. Our findings converged to suicide. Due to a simple bureaucratic detail, Da Costa refused to sign it. That does not invalidate the document."

As he heard Lavradio, Rubens remembered how surprised he had been when he read the conclusion of the investigation: too simple, effortless. There seemed to be no interest in verifying the facts. That piece of paper gave him the vivid impression of a complete forgery. But who was he to confront the ambitions of high officials?

"I read you loud and clear. He'll see you in your office tomorrow at 2 p.m."

On Tuesday afternoon, Marcelo reported to Chief Jose Lavradio.

He heard a litany of frail arguments whose purpose was to explain how they concluded that the sergeant had committed suicide. Moreover, the matter was hushed up to avoid exploitation by the media with dire consequences for the government's public image. Marcelo pretended to understand and agree. He promised to limit his investigation of the watchman's murder to local circumstances within the residential complex. He even went so far as to say that his clues were consistently leading him to the conclusion that the old man had accidentally fallen into the well. "He must've been plastered," he added. As for the murder of the couple, there was no connection whatsoever. Incidentally, he was going to ask Chief Rubens to be relieved from the double murder case, since he had not yet wrapped up the other one.

Back at the precinct, he was welcomed with good tidings by Chief Rubens. Marcelo had just been transferred to the State Police Intelligence Bureau. Quite a promotion; he was moving on up the ladder of success within the force. Only the most capable agents ended up in that billet.

"You can report over there for duty tomorrow," Rubens said. "You'll be working for Chief Carlos Estevao, the pope of police intelligence."

"I'm flabbergasted, sir, I really am… and honored of course," Marcelo stuttered. "Did you give them my name, sir?"

"I didn't. I just answered a couple of questions about you, is all. Someone with the president's staff pulled your name off the list. Got any friend or patron among the gods up on Mount Olympus?"

"Not exactly a friend; much less a patron… but I got along just fine with the members of the staff I talked with," he exaggerated.

Back at his desk, he tried to compose himself and deal with the news. The adrenaline had taken its toll on him since he had heard about his promotion. He did his best to look nonchalant and avoid a feeling of resentment among his colleagues aroused by his good fortune. He had long nursed the ambition of one day becoming a member of the Intelligence Agency, where the cream of the crop in the force was. His transference had another great advantage to boot: he would be getting rid of the awkward situation of having to dig up the evidence and seeing to the indictment of the insurance broker Sergio Gomes who was to take the blame for the double assassination that he, Marcelo Moreira, had committed himself. He smiled when he remembered how easy it had been to carry out his revenge; not to mention his satisfaction in rigorously punishing the man who had dared compete with him for the love of Jandira. With the malignant intent of rubbing in his triumph and the poor fellow's disgrace, he decided to pay Sergio a visit in jail on that very afternoon. He intended to promise Sergio that he would do his best to get him off the hook, but he actually wanted to sneer at the stressed-out cretin who had deprived him of the company of Jandira by taking her out on dates or to barbecues at some stupid relative's house or stalking her at her workplace every single day. Sergio, in Marcelo's warped mind, was an imbecile in love who coveted a woman who was way beyond his limited range.

"What the hell are you doing here?" said Sergio when he saw Marcelo who did not expect such a poor welcome; but soft-spoken Marcelo "Sweet Lip" Moreira never altered his tone of voice; neither did he ever show any emotion. He was always polite.

"Chill out, my good man! I come as a friend and in good will. I know you're not guilty of anything. You were framed and fell for it. I promise to find out who made up the evidence and contrived events so as to incriminate you falsely."

"Get the fuck out of here!" Sergio raved, staring at Marcelo and grasping the cell bars with both hands. "I don't need your frigging help!"

Sweet Lip never said goodbye. He just turned his back on the broker and left, thinking: "This whoreson bastard suspects me. Well, that's how he'll go down the drain; there's no way he can incriminate me."

Marcelo returned to the precinct where he gathered his belongings, put them in his backpack, said goodbye to his colleagues, went home, donned a jacket and tie, and headed for the Intelligence Agency.

He went up to the third floor and reported to the man in charge, Director Carlos Estevao.

"It's a pleasure to have you with us," said Estevao.

Addressing the policeman at his side, Estevao handed him a folder: "Ricardo, this is detective Marcelo Moreira. He's joining our team. "Show him around, introduce him to his new colleagues, and show him to his desk."

While Marcelo and Ricardo were shaking hands, Estevao said: "Moreira, tomorrow, you'll come along with me on a visit to Interpol. We'll join a meeting to be held at 3 p.m. with representatives of Sao Paulo and Portugal police departments. They've come to Brasília in pursuit of a terrorist. You'll have a chance to see how we work with the feds."

Marcelo was introduced to his new colleagues before he was left at his new desk.

He pulled his things out of the backpack, arranging them on his new desk and in the drawers. He turned on the computer and mused as he ran the mouse over the links. "I never thought this agency had anything to do with the Interpol, especially to exchange notes on terrorists. Terrorists in Brasília? I could swallow that, if they were talking most wanted traffickers, corrupt cops, sold-out judges, embezzling businessmen, thieving bankers, and graft-involved public servants, that is, the usual pack of white-collar rogues that blend right in with the elite of this country. But terrorists? They've got to be kidding!"

He locked up his desk drawers, shut off the desktop, and went home.

Marcelo woke up early on Thursday morning. He took a shower, donned a jacket and tie, and went by his former precinct before heading for the Intelligence Agency. He ran into Luiz.

"Who's been assigned to replace me in the double murder case?"

"Detective Lacerda, but he hasn't come in yet."

"What about the watchman we found at the bottom of that well?"

"The boss pulled the curtain on it. Case's closed. He said a blind man could see it was an accident."

Marcelo read between the lines and sensed the invisible hand of the president's staff shaping the progress and altering the due course of events. They did not want the truth. Indeed, in his interview with Lavradio he had noticed the satisfaction in the chief's eyes, when he told him about his suspicion that the old man had accidentally fallen into the well. "The watchman must've been plastered," he said.

"I bet he based his decision to close the case on my fib," he thought to himself.

"Is Lacerda coming to work today?" Marcelo asked. "I need to see him."

Luiz checked his watch.

"I reckon he is. Should be here by now."

"I can only wait ten minutes. I'm swamped by work," Marcelo lied, since he had not yet met his sponsor who was going to show him the ropes for his new job description. "What about the boss, is he here?"

"Sure is. Why don't you go right in and pay your respects. I'll let Lacerda know you're here to see him."

Rubens told him that Lacerda intended to drop by the agency to talk to him about the cases he had inherited.

Rubens handed him a brief.

"When you're done reading it, talk to Lacerda."

Moreira sat down in an easy chair across from the chief's desk and glanced through the document. There was nothing new. His own suspicions about Sergio Gomes, the broker, had been printed in proper police jargon. It closed with the recommendation that a search be undertaken in the pickup and apartment of the suspect. "They found nothing that might incriminate me," he thought. "I did everything right, and they fell for it. There's nothing to worry about."

He got back on his feet and put the file on the desk.

"So there it is, sir" Marcelo said. "Well written, concise, thorough. I have nothing to add. You know me, sir. I'm at your service if you need me for anything at all. Just give me a call and I'll be there in a jiffy."

"That's so very true," said Rubens as they shook hands. "Thanks for your cooperation."

As he was walking down the hall towards the exit he bumped into Detective Lacerda coming in.

"I came over to see you," said Marcelo. "Maybe you need to know something from me about the case… something I may have left out."

In spite of his portly figure, Lacerda walked with ease. Bald and bearded, his fair skin was tanned by the tropical sun. His blue eyes gave away the European strain in him. His booming voice echoed in the hallway.

"My good friend Sweet Lip, you're a sight for sore eyes!" he whooped.

They hugged.

"No sooner I came back from vacation than they shied a double murder at me," Lacerda said. "I guess I lucked out, though, since you've already found out who done it. You know, you totally deserve that transfer to Intelligence. As far as I know, you're the smartest detective out of the great State of Paraiba yet. How are you, kiddo?"

Marcelo was emotionally moved. Lacerda had a way to call him by his nickname without displeasing him. He decided to use Lacerda's moniker to reciprocate.

"Like I said, Kraut, and I say again: Your wish is my command. Is there anything else you need to clear this mess up? Anything that needs to be added to the inquiry file?"

"No, nothing else, kiddo. Did you read the report?"

"Just a gander when I looked in on the head honcho. He let me leaf through it. When did you write those pages?"

"Yesterday. I reported back. They hit me with it and I immediately started cracking. You'd already left to work alongside of all that extraordinary intellectual and creative power," Lacerda chuckled. "I checked out your old cube and merely copied off the notes you kept in that brown file. I had everything wrapped up by 10 p.m."

"A clean-cut job," Marcelo buttered up. "You're a smooth writer."

"I thought maybe I'd comb the suspect's apartment," Lacerda said. "The warrant's still good. Why waste it? But, since you've already produced the murder weapon, maybe that won't be necessary."

"Go for it by all means," Marcelo stirred him on. "Suppose you come across something. It'll enrich the investigation record. The more, the merrier."

Marcelo knew that a search at the insurance broker's home would not expose him or make him liable to suspicion.

Nothing would be found. It might even divert away the course of the investigation.

He left the precinct feeling calm and secure.

While driving to his new workplace, he devised for the umpteenth time a list of self-satisfying reasons for his behavior and weighed the possibilities that the truth would be revealed. "I've just committed the perfect crime," he mused.

He was whistling a song as he walked towards his desk at the agency. No sooner had he started fiddling with his computer than Agent Tiago materialized in front of him.

"You must be our most recent addition," said an uninhibited Tiago. "Detective Moreira, right?"

Marcelo got up from his chair.

"In the flesh. I'm pleased to meet you."

"I'm Tiago. You just sit there, and I'll sit over here," said Tiago, pulling up a chair. "Listen closely! I'll tell you everything there is to know. It's no big deal."

For over an hour Tiago went over documents and reports with Marcelo, hammering data and information into his head. Then they went out to lunch together. When they returned, everything that had been said was summarized. Tiago asked some questions to test Marcelo's aptitude. He was impressed with the detective's newly-acquired knowledge and mental faculty for retaining it.

"You've got a highly-developed memory. You're apt to act independently and work by yourself. Let me know if you have any doubts."

Tiago got up and walked off without another word.

Two blocks past the building where the office of the insurance broker Sergio Gomes was located, there was a small police station exclusively for foreign tourists. At the very same moment as Marcelo and Commissioner Carlos Estevao were on their way to the Interpol office for a meeting with a couple of agents from Sao Paulo who were on the trail of a terrorist, a flannel boy approached the reception desk at this small police station. He had a newspaper in his hand.

"Officer, I wish to report a felony."

The policemen gave him a reproachful look. That was no tourist, to be sure.

"We only handle tourists here. You'll have to speak with an accent, or else go seek the shelter of some other place of worship. Take your issue up to the 13th Precinct on North Superblock Six. It's the nearest one. Unless your complaint has anything to do with tourists. Well, does it?"

"No sir. I keep an eye on the cars parked around this neighborhood. I clean them out and wash them, too."

"I see. You're a goddamned flannel boy. So what?"

The flannel boy pointed at Detective Marcelo Moreira's picture in the newspaper.

"I read in this here paper that Mr. Sergio… Well, Mr. Sergio is a chummy black man who owns a business down the street where I operate. I take good care of his car… He didn't…"

"Slow down! Get to the point," the policeman cut in. "What seems to be the problem?"

"That's what I'm driving at, officer. You see, like I said, Mr. Sergio was accused of shooting that couple, just 'cause they found a pistol in his pickup, I mean, under the driver's seat… That's what is written here. Well, it so happens that I saw this man here, see?" He stuck his index finger in Marcelo's picture. "He was tampering with Mr. Sergio's pickup, see? Every Monday and Thursday, very early in the morning, Mr. Sergio leaves the pickup door unlocked so I can clean and vacuum the interior. On that day, I cleaned the dashboard, the seats and under the seats like I always do. I saw no gun anywhere.

There was no gun to be seen. Then I took a break and had a sandwich while watching the cars. This man," again he pointed at Marcelo's picture, "opened the car door, did something with his hands inside the vehicle, and closed it again." He scratched his head in a nervous gesture. "Before he tampered with that seat, there was no gun in that pickup, I'm telling you…"

The policeman was quite taken aback by that statement and utterly curious to hear out the rest of it.

"Hold it! Hold it" he exclaimed with his palm up. "Please run that by me again! You're quite sure you saw this man," he pointed at the paper, "sticking his hands into the nice black man's automobile and then what?…" He asked and stood there staring at the flannel boy.

"It ain't no automobile. It's a pickup. Like I said…" He repeated the whole story.

The policeman came out from behind the counter.

"Come on!" he gestured. "I want you to repeat this in front of the chief."

They walked over to the door of a small office where a gray-haired, green-eyed man was speaking on the phone. The flannel boy was shivering from head to toe.

"What seems to be the problem, Euclides?" he asked as he hung up the phone. "Come on in!"

"Boss, this flannel boy's been singing an interesting tune. He's kinda jittery, though. Sounds like serious business, real heavy stuff."

"Thank you, Euclides. You may go, now! Take a seat over there, young man!" The chief gestured to a chair. "Let's hear it from the top!"

"I look after the parked cars along this street, sir. I'm a flannel boy, but I've got a permit from the City to do it, sir."

He stuck his hand in his pocket, pulled out a greasy old card with his faded photograph on it and handed it over to the chief. The policeman barely glanced at the permit and returned it to him.

"What's your name?"

"My name's Antonio, sir, Antonio Serafim, but everybody calls me Toninho."

All that trembling and cold-sweating drew out the chief's compassion.

"Chill out, boy!" Nothing to be scared about!"

"Yes, sir. I'm kinda of ill at ease…" The flannel boy shrank back into his seat, rubbed his hands together, blushed and smiled. "Please forgive me!"

The lawman pulled out a pack of cigarettes and offered him one.

"No, thanks, sir. I don't smoke."

"Feel more relaxed now?" the lawman asked after taking a drag and puffing out smoke.

"Yes, sir, I reckon I am."

"OK, then. We can talk now. Tell me your story."

Toninho repeated what he had said to officer Euclides. The chief refrained from putting pressure on him.

"I admire your courage," the lawman said soothingly. "You came in here and made very serious accusations, involving a policeman. Aren't you afraid of reprisals?

"I am, sir, but… You see, Your Excellency, Mr. Sergio pays me to clean his pickup inside out on Mondays and Thursdays. He always gives me a good tip on the side. If he goes to jail, it'll cut down on my income. We're talking my livelihood here. Besides, everything I said is gospel truth. I'm ready to swear to this, Your Honor.

"Anybody else saw him tamper with the car?"

"It's a big pickup, sir. It's not just a car."

"Whatever! Did anybody else besides you see all this?"

"Mr. Clovis, the drycleaner, saw it, too. He took a good gander at him," the flannel boy said, pointing at the newspaper.

The lawman got up from his chair.

"Come along with me!" he said to Toninho.

The next room had a chair close to an intercom.

"Sit down over here," he said pulling up the chair and reaching for the intercom.

"Sonia," he spoke into the machine. "This is Madeira. Get over here, please!"

A plump, short, dark policewoman materialized at the door.

"Give this young man some cold water and hot coffee! Entertain him while I make a phone call."

He went back into his room, closing the door behind him, and dialed a number.

"This is Jose Madeira, foreign tourist precinct. I need to speak with Commissioner Rubens.

He was immediately aware of the impact of his words on Rubens.

"Are you sure your informant was talking about Marcelo Moreira?"

"Absolutely, but he isn't my informant. He has a newspaper with Marcelo Moreira's photograph. He's scared shitless."

There was a long pause in the conversation.

"This is amazing to me!" Rubens said finally. "Moreira of all detectives! But here's what we'll do… He is very popular among his colleagues, and there is a great deal of corporatism here, as you probably know already. I'm talking about a community based upon a strong organic social and functional solidarity. I kid you not. So I think you'd better call Rauster in Internal Affairs and ask him to assign somebody to take a statement from this flannel boy over there in your ball park. What do you think?"

Madeira was silent for a moment before he answered.

"Yeah, I guess you're right. I'll give him a buzz right now."

Before Madeira could hang up, he had to hear out Rubens, who droned on about how surprised he was that one of his best detectives might be involved in such a disgusting plot. "I'm praying it turns out to be a mistake or some sort of misunderstanding," he said, "although my vast experience, during all these years in the force, has taught me that the fiercest hearts are often in those we least suspect."

Madeira ran his finger down the list under the glass cover of his desk until he stopped at a number which he dialed. After a short telephone call he came out of his office.

"Sit tight and enjoy Sonia's company," he told the flannel boy. "An agent from Internal Affairs is on his way to hear you out."

Noticing that Toninho was still frightened and again had started to break out in a cold sweat, the lawman tried to restore his confidence. "All you have to do is to tell him the same thing you told me just to go on the record. And don't forget to mention that fellow Clovis, the drycleaner. He, too, will be heard. After that mum's the word. Remember that discretion is paramount."

Madeira went back into his office, sat down at his desk, and lit a cigarette. He was worried. By formally accusing the detective, the flannel boy was putting his own life on the line. He rated the boy's courage highly. Actually, Madeira was growing fond of him. The way the flannel boy protected his business interests with a complete disregard for the risks involved reminded him of his own poor, toilsome childhood. He had to struggle to get where he was. Suddenly a smile broke out wide across his face as he remembered his own savvy to make a fast buck. It happened when he was a teenager and found a baby macaw near his home at the time when the city of Brasilia was still under construction.

Those were the days when there was no legal restriction on caging, buying, selling, or consuming wildlife. He raised the creature that grew into a large bird with a huge tail. Boisterous and ravenous, it preyed upon the fruits in the house, climbed up to the higher places, and soiled everything it touched. To keep it from flying away and escaping, one of the bird's legs was tied to a 30-foot-long nylon string attached to the pantry table. His mother would go crazy over the squawks and the racket. Time and again she would take Queen's— that what he named the parrot— mischievousness out on him. He himselfcould no longer put up with the bird's capers, but he feared that it might become an easy prey to predators if he were to set it free. He was very fond of Queen.

One day, he came up with an idea.

In Brasilia there was a pet shop in the mall. He got hold of their phone number and called them from a public phone booth.

"Do you have a macaw for sale?"

"No, we don't. Macaws are trouble. Not much demand, if any."

Three days later, young Madeira called them up again and stuck to this practice every other day with the same question, altering his voice and improvising on his lines. "I'm in dire need of a macaw" or "I'm willing to pay a good price," and so forth.

Three weeks later he put the bird on a perch and took it to the mall. As he was leisurely walking past the pet shop, the manager saw him.

"How much do you want for that macaw?"

"You wanna buy my parrot?" the boy asked him with an expression of pure innocence on his face.

"Oh, yes. I have a few customers who are very much interested."

"She's not for sale."

"I can make a pretty generous offer, you know?"

"I'll think about it."

"There's nothing to think about, boy," said the manager, offering to pay so handsome a sum that the boy had to control himself to avoid suspicion.

The deal was closed and two months went by. One morning he passed by the shop and saw that Queen, however shackled and shrieking from time to time, had gained weight and seemed to be well-treated.

"I hope nobody tries to hurt this kid," Madeira muttered after he was done reminiscing, while crushing his cigarette into an ashtray.

One hour later, investigator Celio Oliveira from Internal Affairs arrived at the precinct. He took the flannel boy's statement and complied with all the legal formalities. After Toninho signed the document they both headed for the drycleaner's. The manager, Clovis Silva, had just come in when they got there.

Celio flashed his badge and asked him whether he knew the flannel boy.

"This boy? Why, sure I do. He's Toninho. I know him all right. What's he done?"

"Nothing. He didn't do anything. He said he was sitting on a stool right outside your place and you were standing not far from him when both of you saw this man"— he showed Marcelo's picture in the paper— "nosing into an insurance broker's pickup…"

"Mister Sergio Gomes," Toninho complemented.

"Right! Sergio Gomes. Do you confirm this?"

Clovis looked at the photograph and read the caption. When he learned the man was a cop, he backed down in fear.

"No… No, no. I… don't remember any of this."

"Take a good look at this photo," the policeman said. "Here, hold the paper in your hands."

Clovis stared at Marcelo Moreira's face. His hands were trembling.

"I've never seen this man in my life," he finally said, returning the newspaper to the investigator.

"Come on! Let's go down to the station together."

"Right now?"

"Sure. We need to talk."

Clovis asked his wife to mind the shop and stepped out with Celio. He was scared.

Only around 8 p.m., after much insistence from the investigator and a promise of absolute secrecy, the drycleaner began to break down.

"Look, officer," he said, "I'm a married man with four children. I find it very dangerous to stick to this story. I've been told that he who messes with a lawman flirts with death. Even with your promise that nothing's going to happen to me, I'm still stricken with the greatest fear. I've never been this afraid before."

"Listen up! They want to keep this thing under wraps. That's why I 've been assigned to investigate this here detective. And I'll tell you why, too. Because that way he'll never know we're wise to him, see? Besides, all witnesses are protected for the same reason. You follow?"

Clovis read and re-read his statement. He looked at the clock on the wall, then in Celio's face and again at the document he held in his hand. He was shivering in fear. He wiped his face with a handkerchief, cleared his throat, and read the statement all over again.

Celio was leaning against the wall, his arms crossed.

"Be it as it may, you'll be subpoenaed. You'll have to appear in court to give your testimony, either for the defense or the prosecution," he said, shrugging.

Clovis looked up, frowning.

"Defense or prosecution? I don't get it."

"If you sign it, there'll be no doubt that you'll testify for the prosecution. If you don't and, for that reason, the judge gets the wrong idea, you may be considered an accomplice trying to cover for a criminal. The bottom line is that there'll be a lot of suspicion regarding your attitude, in view of the testimony of the other witness.

Clovis sat down and signed the paper.

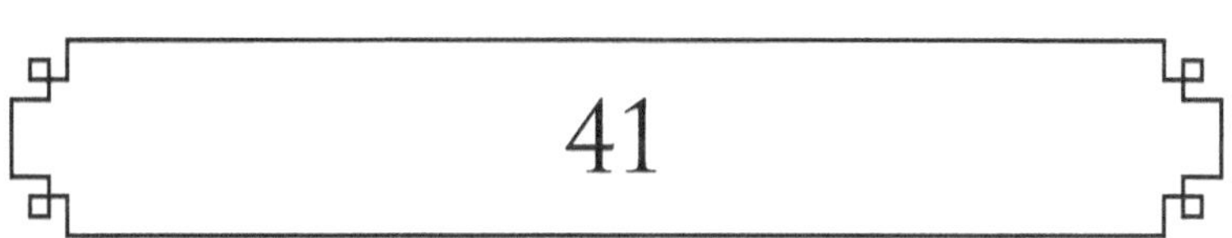

The meeting scheduled to begin at 3:00 p.m. at the Interpol headquarters was convened two hours and ten minutes later. "I thought things around here functioned within a formal, efficient, methodical structure as in the coordination and direction of activities," Marcelo was thinking as he was herded into a packed conference hall with Chief Carlos Estevao and other guests.

Sitting in the chair on the row immediately behind his new boss, Marcelo inspected critically the cold, expressionless décor when his attention was driven off to the entrance of a tall, slim man with a full head of hair, wearing old-fashioned spectacles. Right behind him was a beautiful, slender woman followed by a European-looking gentleman elegant in dress and appearance.

"Good-afternoon, ladies and gentlemen!"

"Good afternoon!" was the greeting chorus.

"I guess almost everyone here knows me. Anyway, allow me to introduce myself to casual first-timers. I am Commissioner Norton Placido, head of Interpol in Brazil. Here at my side, I have Interpol agent Raquel Lopes from our branch in Sao Paulo. This gentleman is detective Mauricio Santana from the Lisbon Police Department. They're both trailing a terrorist who committed a murder in Portugal. He killed 19-year-old, eh…"— he read the name off a small piece of paper— "Eduardo Santana who was Detective Santana's brother"— he gestured at Mauricio— "and the fact of the matter is that the thread of this investigation is leading us to suspect the existence of other terrorists in this country who are trying to establish an al-Qaeda network in Brazil…"

Meanwhile, Gamal sat waiting for Hassan at the refuge. They had agreed to go over the plan one last time, especially the sequence of all possible contingent procedures in view of the guest-list layout on the flight deck of the aircraft carrier. He took time to reflect and speculate on the visit Detective Marcelo Moreira had paid to the gym to snoop around about Sergeant Deivid. It was getting on his nerves. He had never brought Deivid up with his accomplice, so there was no way Hassan could know anything about their classes or anything else.

"Then how did the cops hear about it?" he asked himself.

Always attentive to potential danger and extremely suspicious by nature, Gamal decided to stay in Brasilia only until the coming Friday. Considering how unpredictable Hassan had proved to be, the terrorist needed to be sure that he would not have second thoughts when push came to shove.

There was of course no way of knowing beforehand whether Hassan would follow through on his intent to carry out his personal vengeance as planned. Nevertheless, Gamal decided to place a telephone call on Friday morning to the presidential palace and ask for Hassan. He would say he was speaking on behalf of the gym about a change in the class schedule. If they told him that he had traveled with the president, it would be a reliable sign that Hassan's plan still held for blowing the infidels to kingdom come. If the plan went sour because Hassan failed to carry it to completion, Gamal would arrange for a meeting right there at the refuge when he would kill Hassan and call it a day. Inasmuch as he could not get rid of Detective Moreira, the best course of action afterwards was to get out of Brasilia, out of Brazil.

So absorbed was Gamal in his musings, that he only took notice of Hassan's presence when the motorcycle pulled up close to him.

"Hello there, pard? How goes it?" asked Hassan in a jovial mood.

Gamal was startled.

"Huh?... Me? You... I'm fine."

"What is this? Did I frighten you? Is there a problem?"

"I was deep in thought. Why?"

"I don't know! You seem jumpy."

"Nothing like that. Like I said, I was turning our plan over in my head. I'm sure everything will be just dandy."

"Sure hope so! Well, eh..." the jovial tone was gone. "As a matter of fact, I didn't even need to come out here this evening."

The terrorist felt a chill run down his spine. "Here comes the wacko with another one of his capers," he thought. "Anything wrong with the boy?" he asked.

"Why do you ask that?" said Hassan, trying to disguise the anxiety the question had roused in him.

"Take it easy, my friend!" Gamal reacted. "Don't get all riled up! I meant nothing by it. It's not what you're thinking."

"Hey, friend, I'm not *thinking* anything. What makes you say that?"

"You know what? You're right. I've been mulling over our plan myself, you know, and I… Well, I really think we don't need to go over it anymore. I'm here just to say good-bye. And since you're also so cocksure we don't really need to talk about this at length any longer. I only wish to remind you of the important moves: pull firmly on the ring, remember that fifty seconds later the bomb will go off no matter what, and don't forget to position yourself as close as possible to the American president. Do not let anyone between you two. As for the rest, I agree with you. Let's just bid our farewells. Take a seat over here!"

They sat down on the sand.

Smiling, Gamal took a long look at Hassan, once again savoring his victory over him. He had succeeded in catechizing Hassan, thanks to the hatred he felt for the killers of his family. Had the motive been any other, the plan would never work out, because it would be useless and, to a certain extent, risky to try to talk Hassan into going on with it. Hassan's great loss had made him lose his mental balance. Inherently shy, destitute and riddled with deadly hostility, all he needed was a slight push. He was not like Gamal, not by a long shot. Gamal was evil by nature and in practice; a terrorist radically engaged in the use of force or violence against innocent lives with the intention of intimidating or coercing societies or governments for absurd, hideous and incomprehensible religious reasons. Gamal did this out of sheer wickedness. Hassan was persuaded to perform the attack in the name of a personal cause that was sacred only to him. Hassan did this out of a temporary, mental derangement.

Gamal gave vent to his joy.

"You will be blessed by Allah Himself and He will take you to Heaven!" he prophesied. "In the company of your fiancée Raissa, you'll be able to enjoy a blissful happiness the sort of which does not exist on this confounded, troubled and forlorn planet. The magnitude of your sacrifice is immeasurable and remarkably greater than any attachment to life. You'll never be forgotten by the good souls of mankind."

Hassan kept his eyes fixed on Gamal, while his brain digested the meaning of those words that sounded almost like a lecture bundled up in gratifying praise. The terrorist expressed his judgments in a dogmatic way like an oracle, in his best elocutionary way, and his words glowed with certainty and confidence: a true gift from Allah.

Hassan got up and thanked him.

It was the last time they would ever see each other.

Gamal stood up silently and silently they walked to their respective bikes. The stillness was soon broken by the revving of the engines. Pulling ahead, Hassan raised aloft his right hand, making the V sign for victory.

42

In conclusion of his talk, Commissioner Norton pointed out the Triple Frontier on a map of Brazil and asked Raquel to reveal the evidence she and her partner had uncovered in Iguazu Falls and Iasci.

Enraptured with the beauty and nimbleness of the policewoman, Marcelo Moreira paid little attention to her words. His mind digressed far from the issue at hand. "This babe shouldn't be messing with imaginary terrorists. She's wasting her precious time and she could easily find better use for it. That partner of hers, the stuck-up *porkchop*, probably has an edge over this whole business. I bet he's bagging her. How stupid of me to imagine that Interpol and the Secret Service could come up with any concrete results. What are they thinking? Maybe I put my foot in it when I accepted to work for this band of dreamers. By golly, where do they get this notion that a threat that only exists on the other side of the world, I mean, in the Middle East… Europe and probably the United States… I mean why don't they try to fight off our dire reality as far as bad guys are concerned? Brazil is crawling with them. Terrorists in Brazil… yeah, right! Well, perhaps only in the minds of people with nothing to do, or who don't want to do anything, or don't know any better."

Then Marcelo was taken aback when, out of the blue, piercing through the fog of his rumination, a photograph of Gamal flashed back at him from a slide projected on a large screen. That was the guy he had met at the gym. He felt a sudden chill.

"This is the man we've been tracking down."

This time, Raquel's voice cut through him like a bolt of lightning. Marcelo was thrilled. He sprang up from his seat and raised his arm.

"Any question?" Raquel asked.

By then he had already reassumed the quiet personality of Mr. Sweet Lip.

"I know this man!" he exclaimed. His voice was low, but it carried right through the auditorium.

An almost tangible silence spread across the audience. All eyes converged on the figure of that stranger wearing a visitor tag around his neck.

"Come on down here, please," Norton said to him.

Marcelo joined the group up front, his wobbly legs struggling successfully to quell the excitement. Before anyone questioned him, he introduced himself.

"I'm agent Marcelo Moreira from the State Police Intelligence. Until yesterday I was a detective in the Homicide Division. I was in charge of an investigation into the murder of a watchman in the course of which I questioned that man."—He gestured at the slide— "He's a coach at a martial arts academy hereabouts."

A general buzz engulfed the auditorium.

"Let's hold it down, please!" Norton commanded.

By and by the audience was quiet.

"Are you sure you know this terrorist?" Norton asked Marcelo.

"Absolutely! I actually met him. We had a conversation. Even though his Portuguese is quite fluent I couldn't help noticing a certain foreign accent." He paused to take a long look at the slide. "That's him all right!"

Norton addressed Carlos Estevao, smiling.

"I reckon your boy will have to bear a hand so we can lay our hands on this terrorist. I hope you're willing to rent him out."

Estevao smiled as he got up and joined the group up front.

"Agent Marcelo Moreira brought luck to my department, but I'll let you borrow him for free."

Again the drone of voices filled the room. For a few minutes there was a murmur of simultaneous conversations with exchange of opinions and suggestions. The joke was on Marcelo who basked in the glory of being the center of attraction, yielding smiles all around and giving a false appearance of bashfulness. Servers came in with coffee and cookies. Ten minutes went by before Norton managed to reassume control.

"OK, people, please go back to your seats, and try to refrain from making any more noises. Let's focus here."

Then he addressed Raquel and Mauricio.

"We know that we've got your man in sight. If he hasn't made his escape yet, we'll get him for sure. Any suggestion?"

"Mr. Commissioner," said Mauricio, "terrorists are very elusive and extremely suspicious. The slightest hint that we're on to him will make him vanish into thin air. We should make the arrest immediately, and I mean right now."

These words caused an excited, noisy activity in the auditorium, and once more the whir of busy voices expressed different views and reactions: some wanted to raid the gym at once, some thought it would be better to get prepared first and go for it tomorrow, and some wanted to wait for the terrorist at his place of residence.

And once again Norton had to intervene.

"OK, you guys, listen up! This man can try to make a break for it at any moment now. Therefore, I believe it's best to accept the suggestion offered by our Portuguese colleague. There are also security reasons for this course of action, since we don't know what the terrorist is up to. You know the routine… I mean, the longer we wait… Well, anyway I'm going to call out the special operations squad to bear a hand, and I'll assign one of you to be in charge. Any volunteer?"

Almost all present raised a hand.

Norton smiled and decided to pick out the most senior agent in the house, Tadeu Rezende.

"He's too old for this, boss. Look at him, sir, he's pushing 100 and crumbling down," said Agent Juliano who liked to tease his colleagues, bringing on a roar of male laughter.

"Stick it in your ear!" Tadeu shot back.

The meeting was adjourned. Everybody was dismissed except those who would take part in the raid and Marcelo Moreira.

"Congratulations! I wish you luck, but be careful!" Commissioner Carlos Estevao said to Marcelo before the left.

Marcelo retold his story to Tadeu, Raquel and Mauricio, adding details of his talk with the receptionist at the gym. He knew that instructor Gamal— Raquel and Mauricio exchanged glances at the sound of the terrorist's name— lived at hotel

Bajara in the outskirts of Brasília, near the paved road that led to Taguatinga. It was an isolated building at a forked crossing where another side road split up. "By a fortunate coincidence, I know exactly where it is," Marcelo added. The coach taught his classes every morning on weekdays from seven to noon and at night from seven to ten.

Armed with this information Tadeu Rezende summoned the commandant of the Special Operations Squad and invited the agents involved to take their seats around the long, rectangular table in the briefing room adjacent to the auditorium.

"As soon as the commandant gets here, we will plan this thing out. The scene of action will be the hotel where the terrorist is staying. Agent Marcelo here says there are usually very few guests. It's less dangerous than the gym."

Then he addressed Marcelo.

"I want you to pass by the gym and check whether the target's still there teaching his classes. Before you leave, stop off by Personnel and ask for Agent Henrique Sousa to be assigned to go with you. Brief him on the way over. The terrorist knows you, but he's never seen Sousa. Stake him out and don't lose him. Here are the numbers of my two cell phones. Keep me posted of your whereabouts all the time. Take one of our unmarked squad cars with fake license plates. It's a good thing you know where the hotel is located. When this Gamal is done teaching, you guys stay on his ass, but don't let him notice he's being followed. Let me know whether he's really heading for the hotel or wherever. Now, listen up. I say again: keep me posted of every move this SOB makes, constantly, you hear? What's your cell phone number? Another thing, you and Sousa work as a team, you hear?"

As Marcelo Moreira was leaving, he heard Raquel's voice: "Good luck, companion!"

"That would be up to you, Baby, wouldn't it now?" he thought with a mischievous grin. "I wish I could get that lucky!"

He passed by the Personnel Division. Sousa was there, waiting for him. Tadeu had called ahead.

Standing outside the gym with Sousa, Marcelo saw through the huge glass wall that Gamal was engaged in a conversation with the receptionist.

"That's him by the reception desk," Marcelo said. "Can you see him?"

"Yeah. It's not hard to commit that ugly Arab face to memory."

"OK then," said Marcelo. "I'll wait in the car. We don't want him to see me; and since he doesn't know you, you can go in and act like you intend to join up, or are looking for somebody, or just want to take a whiz. Just don't lose him. Keep your eyes fixed on his ass, OK?"

"No problem. Run along back to the car. By the way, where's his bike?"

"Come with me!"

Marcelo showed him the motorcycle and went back to the car. He sat there behind the wheel and watched as Sousa walked into the gym."

43

While the Interpol team was working on a plan to arrest Gamal, the terrorist stepped into the mosque, said his prayers, once again thanked Allah for making Hassan come his way, and went to the gym.

He stopped off at the reception desk. "Has that cop been looking for me again?" he asked.

"No, coach, he hasn't. He only came over that one time," the girl replied.

"Did he ever ask anything about me?"

"Not much. When I told him he had just missed you, he asked for your address, and I had to give it to him. It's the law. Bajara Hotel, right? But he told me the hotel was too far, and it would work better for him to come back and talk to you here. And so he did, at night, when you had classes. I saw you two chatting."

"So you gave him my address," Gamal muttered more to himself than to the receptionist."

"Like I said, I had to. Are you saying I shouldn't have?"

"No, no, by no means! Everything's just fine. Thanks!"

Agent Sousa saw Gamal go into the locker room, where he separated the items that he intended to carry with him on the next morning, when he would make his escape after placing that call to the palace.

Gamal donned his uniform and headed for the tatami, where he taught two classes. He asked his assistant to take over the last one for him. "I'm going back to the hotel. I'm not feeling well tonight at all." He climbed on his motorcycle and drove away. He never noticed that far, behind, a car was trailing him. A few minutes after Gamal pulled up in front of the Bajara, the car with Agent Sousa behind the wheel rolled by towards Taguatinga. Sitting next to him Marcelo punched numbers on his cellphone. "He's in," he said into the mouthpiece and hung up without waiting for a reply.

Gamal greeted Nice, the clerk at the front desk of the hotel's tiny reception room.

When she became a widow, Vitoria Bajara, the owner, laid off all her employees, keeping only Sebastiao, dubbed Tiao, a dour half-breed who handled all the daily chores and, in the early years of her widowhood, was also her lover. She also kept two young ladies, Nice and Neide. They took turns at the front desk during the night shift. In addition, a cleaning lady also acted as cook and did other menial tasks from 7 a.m. through 7 p.m.

Good old Vitoria took care of everything else.

Vitoria sat at the front desk during the day. She was a little over eighty years old and had no children. She was well aware that her life was at its ebb and pondered her preferences on who should inherit her decaying property frequented by prostitutes, drunkards, drug dealers, thieves, swindlers, and pimps. Her prices were way below market rates when compared to the filthiest joints in that area. Vitoria was sorry she could not leave the hotel to Tiao, who, however many years younger, was now a frail man consumed by a cancer that would probably kill him before she died. The hotel had six rooms on the ground floor and eight more upstairs. There were two guests who lived in the hotel: a wildlife trafficker and Gamal. The trafficker, as usual, was away on one of his many trips all over the state, acquiring and smuggling exotic, rare birds. The other guests were couples who came and went around the clock, mostly hookers with their tricks.

The terrorist went to his room on the second floor, threw his backpack on the bed, opened the closet, removed the bag, and started packing. He placed the ceremonial bomb-man's orange extract, white clothes, and his prayer sheet under his only suit, a couple of pants and shirts, socks, underwear, and a pair of shoes. "One day," he mused, "these items will come in handy."

He pulled out the metal case, opened it, and spread its contents on the bed. He left them there, took off his clothes, and stepped into the shower.

Outside, a car was sitting in the distance with the two policemen inside. Marcelo trained his binoculars on the motorcycle parked near the main entrance of the Bajara. When he noticed the light come on in Gamal's room, he passed the word to Tadeu. "The target is in his room."

Gamal let the water run down his body as he tried to figure out what would be another way to make sure that Hassan would not give up at the last moment. Lost in his thoughts and drowned out by the noise of the shower, he did not hear the two policemen who quietly herded the few guests out of the premises. Vitoria turned out to be a problem. She refused to leave. Only dint of a great deal of smooth talk lavished upon her by one of the agents, she finally broke down and decided to comply. Marcelo put her in the back seat of the car, where she soon was sound asleep. The other three couples hurried out into the night, and they were all relieved to know that the cops were not after them, since they all had long criminal records. Tiao was nowhere to be found. He was undergoing chemotherapy at a public hospital in Taguatinga. He had traveled all the previous night and slept on the sidewalk in front of the hospital, with a lengthy line of sick people behind him, all with the desperate hope of getting any treatment at all, for such are the precarious conditions of Brazilian public medical care.

Nice, the receptionist at the front desk, promised to stay there until the police arrived. Her job now was to refuse new guests in case they trickled in. For all purposes there were no vacancies. Moreover, her presence gave the impression that everything was normal, in case Gamal showed up for some reason.

The terrorist finished his shower, and, after drying himself off, he put on shorts and a t-shirt. He carefully returned the items he had left on the bed to the metal case. Then he placed the spare bomb, the big one, on top of everything, leaving the metal case open, because he intended to dismantle the bomb on the next morning and bury the metal case before he fled. It would have to be two trips to the secret spot where he buried his things, inasmuch as he could not at once carry both pieces of luggage on the bike.

There was still one item on the bed. It was a large, thick brown envelope inside a plastic bag. Gamal opened it and counted out the U.S. dollar and euro bills. It was a lot of money.

He put part of it back into the envelope and tossed it into the metal case. He stuffed the rest of the bills into his backpack.

The unmarked police car was about 350 yards from the hotel, half hidden among the lush greenery that surrounded the deserted neighborhood. Inside the vehicle, Vitoria snored, and Sousa dozed off. Outside, behind a tree, his field glasses fixed on the motorcycle, Marcelo Moreira lurked behind a tree. He pressed redial and said: "All set. Only one bird in the nest. Lights on. Will inform when it's off."

Fifty minutes later, the light in the room was turned out. The terrorist hugged the pillow, closed his eyes, and tried to go to sleep.

Again Marcelo Moreira pressed redial.

"Lights out!" he said.

44

As he lurked behind a tree, his eyes fixed on the terrorist's window, sizing up every movement, Marcelo Moreira had a sudden flashback of his first time around at the Bajara Hotel two years before. One morning, returning to Brasilia by bus from Taguatinga, he sat beside an attractive young woman whose long hair had been bleached with peroxide. Being partial to blondes, he struck up a conversation with her. Her name was Helena. She lived in Taguatinga, and, every working day, she would ride the bus to Brasilia to sell costume jewelry and other trinkets, which she carried carefully stowed in a bag, to women public servants in the capital. In the evening she would take the bus back to Taguatinga.

As time went by the couple met a few times in Brasilia and Taguatinga and became good friends. It did not take long for them to begin going steady and seeing each other on an intimate basis.

At that time Marcelo owned an old used car. Every day he would pick her up at 6 p.m. and drive her home. On one of those trips, driven by lust, he pulled up at the Bajara Hotel where they had two hours of passionate sex before moving on to Taguatinga. Ever since that day, this erotic pit stop turned into a routine.

After three months of this customary and often mechanically performed activity, Marcelo was bored. Apart from the fact that it had become weary by being dull, repetitive, and tedious, he was beginning to fret about the cut into his budget caused by the increased spending on gasoline and sex encounters at the Bajara. "Not to mention," he mused, "that this bimbo's performance in the sack isn't a prize package, either."

Marcelo decided to break off the affair.

He started out by making excuses, saying that he was swamped by his police work. "I'm loaded down with cases that I have to handle, Babe. Investigations make me go places, far-off places, see?" He began to be consistently late for their trysts, which were getting fewer and far between. One night, he let her stand there, waiting for him until 8 p.m. The next time around he stood her up.

Finally, Helena had had enough. They broke up.

By then Marcelo was already on a first name basis with Vitoria and her staff at the Bajara. So it follows that it was not so difficult to convince the old hotel owner to sit in the car and wait for the police to lay their hands on the terrorist.

Marcelo went further down memory lane, and he recollected another tragicomic incident which took place in one of the hotel rooms three months after he and Helena had gone their separate ways. Invited by a friend, he joined a group of police officers who wanted to make some money on the side by hiring out to a rancher whose wife had been cheating on him. The rancher, a tall, sturdy man, escorted by the four cops he had hired, sneaked into the Bajara, bribed the clerk, got hold of a master key, and tiptoed upstairs. The rancher was a tall and very strong man. They opened the bedroom door where the rancher's spouse and her lover, the husband's own foreman, were caught naked and in the act, so to speak.

The rancher went berserk. He put up his fists, cursed out the lovers, and advanced towards them with a vengeance and a death wish. One of the cops scoped up the big picture and, having forgotten the rancher's name, he shouted to Marcelo who was closest to the enraged husband.

"Grab the cuckold! Grab the cuckold! Don't let him at the woman!"

In the ensuing chaos the woman was hit by the rancher, who was wildly swinging punches all around. Marcelo himself ended up with a conspicuous black eye. For several days he had to wear a pair of shades, purchased from a street vendor at the bus station in Brasilia. Whenever he ran into one of his colleagues, he heard the same jibe: "Howdy, Sweet Lip! Planning on holding down a cuckold today?"

Leaning against a tree, chuckling at his memories, Marcelo saw the slow-moving procession of police cars approaching with the headlights off. He reached for his cell phone and let Tadeu know where he was. The motorcade formed a single file along the shoulder of the asphalt road. Droves of policemen started spilling out of the vans in dark uniforms, wearing masks and carrying guns over the shoulder or across the chest. It was the GOE, acronym for Special Operations Squad in Portuguese. Tadeu, Raquel, Mauricio, and the drivers had on bulletproof vests. In response to the signals made by their commandant, the uniformed troopers quietly got closer and closer to the hotel. Moreira asked for a bullet proof vest for himself and another for Sousa. He also requested permission to join the GOE team under the excuse of being acquainted with the hotel and knowing the way to the terrorist's room. Permission was granted, but he was supposed to remain two steps behind the commandant and guide him towards the door. It was the commandant's task to make the arrest.

Twelve troopers divided up in groups of three were behind them.

They went in through the reception. Someone told Nice to go sit in the car with Vitoria. They climbed the steps and, guided by Marcelo, arrived at the door of Gamal's room.

Meanwhile, outside, Tadeu, Raquel, Mauricio, Sousa, and the drivers, with guns cocked, positioned themselves behind the vehicles.

The remaining thirty GOE troopers surrounded the Bajara Hotel.

Thinking about the phone call that he would place the next morning to the Palace to make sure that Hassan had traveled with the president's retinue, Gamal was fretting over the execution of his escape plan, and he could not settle himself to sleep. Also, the terrorist's trained senses made him uneasily apprehensive with the unusual, unbroken silence that had settled upon the hotel that night; not even the familiar muffled noises from the other rooms and the street outside could be heard. He sat up in bed and listened for some sort of sound coming from anywhere. Nothing. He silently got out of bed, tiptoed over to the window in the dark and peered out through the blinds. He made out a few crouching shadows quickly closing in on the building. "It's the cops," he murmured. "How the hell did they find me out? It must've been that flatfoot that looked me up at the gym." He reached for the pistol in the metal case and ran for the door. His plan was to flee through the corridor and out the back door before the police could cover the whole perimeter.

It was too late. He got to the door at the exact moment the GOE busted in.

Gamal was quick as a cat. Before they could seize him and hold him down to be cuffed he leaped backwards, jumped on the bed, got hold of the bomb, and pulled the pin.

All hell broke loose. The artifact went off, and so did the grenades, the dynamite sticks, and the C4 explosives that were kept in the metal case. One third of the Bajara went up like an ammunition dump when hit by a shell. Everything else was on fire.

The violent blast was heard for miles all around, including the cities of Brasilia and Taguatinga. Gamal, the GOE commandant, Marcelo, and the twelve troopers in the hallway were killed instantly. Eight of the troopers who surrounded the building died of burns and shrapnel wounds. Three were gravely injured.

Tadeu, Mauricio, Sousa, the drivers, Vitoria, and Nice escaped unscathed. Raquel's hand was hit by a flying piece of debris and her right hand index finger was maimed by a nail. She would never pull a trigger again.

Hassan was lying on a bunk in the dormitory for agents who were required to remain in a state of readiness. He heard the explosion in the distance.

"Something blew up out there, but it wasn't in this town," he whispered to himself.

"I'll tell you one thing," said a colleague on the bunk next to his, "it was no fireworks. Sounds like a plane crash, one of the big ones."

"Keep it down, you guys!" Homero shouted from his bunk in the far end. "We gotta get some rest over here. Tomorrow you'll read and hear about it in the news. Now give me a break, will ya?"

Hassan rolled over, closed his eyes, and went to sleep, dreaming of his forthcoming encounter with the sweet Raissa.

Chief Tadeu Resende was trying to cool down his anger as he watched firemen, paramedics, and state police troopers going about their business in the mayhem created by the explosion. He turned to Commissioner Norton Placido, head of the Interpol in Brazil, who was standing next to him.

"You should never try to seize and hold a terrorist. You just shoot the son of a bitch dead!"

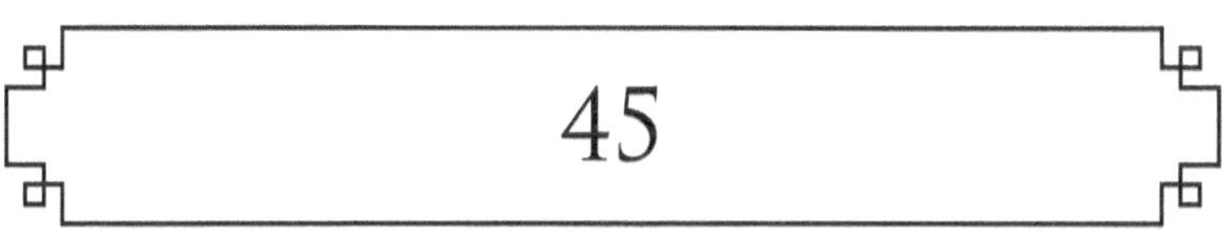

45

President Felipe Ferraro was an intuitive man in a very peculiar way. Since childhood he had developed a faculty for sensing tragedies that were about to happen without the use of any rational process. This sudden, immediate cognition was always preceded by a great, uncontrollable anxiety.

He was never able to banish from his thoughts his recollections of striking events anteceded as a rule by a sense of something not evident or deducible.

He recalled sitting in class of his course in engineering when he was in college and, on and off, having a bad feeling about an oncoming test regardless of how well-prepared he was. It never failed. He got flustered and fretted over some relatively easy calculus problem, making infantile mistakes, wasting precious minutes in the solution of simple, least-valued questions and invariably there would be a number of blank answers when time was up and he had to stop writing and turn in his paper.

Before going into politics he worked as an engineer in the construction of a building. Upon completion, the builder decided to celebrate the event by promoting an opening party. On the eve, Felipe, then unmarried, was unable to sleep at night and had to endure an anxious, unenthusiastic wait for daybreak. Overcome by a vague feeling of bodily discomfort, as at the beginning of an illness, a general sense of unease, he walked to and fro in his room, as though measuring things out while prey to a strange, inexplicable frame of mind. Later on that evening, no sooner had he pulled himself together and arrived at the party than he was given the terrible news: a coworker and dearest friend from college had been killed in a car crash involving a truck while on his way to the same social function.

One year later, following advice from a friend who dealt in the stock exchange and knew a lot of brokers, Ferraro sold the small apartment where he lived and invested all his savings to buy shares in compliance with his friend's counsel. At the time, the stock market was at its peak with most shares on the rise. Blue chips were creating new millionaires overnight.

Advised by a broker friend, Felipe purchased several stocks and, in little over a year, he made a small fortune: six times the value of the apartment he had sold.

When his father, whom he regarded with blind admiration and devotion, learned about his success in the stock market and offered him his congratulations.

"Nothing happens by chance, luck or coincidence, son," the old man said. "You're getting what you deserve, but do not jeopardize it. Stay tuned, because as these achievements are cyclical, they become prone to sudden changes. One day the euphoria will be over, and everything will be the same as before.

Some will come out winners, but others will lose every penny they have. Pray not to be included in the second group."

His old man passed away and Felipe found himself left all alone.

Months later, sitting on a reasonable fortune, Felipe was seized one night by that same anxiety he had grown so accustomed to; only this time, it was far more intense. When he closed his eyes, his father's voice came pounding in his skull like spikes: "Pray not to be included in the second group."

The next day, contrary to the opinion of his broker friend, he converted all his assets into cash by selling off his stocks. In 48 hours the proceeds were deposited into his savings account. In less than a week, the stock market collapsed, ruining the lives of hundreds of investors. Felipe's premonition saved his hide and placed him among the winners of the first group as was his father's wish.

In that same year he decided to go into politics. Next came the rallies, speeches, elections, victory, the glare of the spotlight, and… power.

Felipe partook of the glamour of power.

And with power came flattery, lies, deceit, lust, and especially vanity. He no longer had the time to remember his father's exhortation: "Whenever you feel insecure, confused and indecisive, make a pause, relax, and listen to your heart. From there exudes the correct prompting, the right clue, in the wake of premonition, presentiment, or intuition."

And so the years passed by.

As Felipe advanced in his career, he compromised, little by little, the good values that had always guided his steps. His priorities started to dispense with anything that did not refer to the attainment and application of power. That was when vanity and self-centeredness got the best of him. Political mishaps caused by too much self-regard and immoderation were chalked up to his youth and duly hushed up.

The maturity and experience of the newly-elected president toned down his impulses, and he gradually shaped up into a charismatic leader. Luiza played an important role in his ascent. He managed to maintain constancy of character and purpose in the exercise of his duties thanks in part to the percipient advice and guidance of his wife, always discreet and temperate. Acting from behind the scenes, she used her penetrating clear-sightedness to encourage her husband's initiatives and perfect his performance. At that point, Luiza only admitted long-time friends and supporters into the president's circle, inasmuch as she wanted to cover his back for protection against evil-intentioned politicians who aspired to occupy a place in the shadows, a position of powerful adviser or decision-maker operating secretly, unofficially, acting as an *éminence grise*, so to speak, in the style of Richelieu or Rasputin. She was an educated woman and as such well aware of how dangerous that could be. As a wife she sought first to protect her husband's image; the president's reputation was only her second priority.

The honest truth though was that things were not quite balanced out in Felipe's political and private lives, owing to a few small distortions in his behavior. He seemed to care for nobody short of those who treaded the high spheres. Hence, ignoring Hassan's ordeal came naturally to the President. Hassan was an underling, and Felipe would not waste his precious time with the problems of second stringers. In fact, he had never even spoken to any of his security agents. Luiza had told him about what had happened to Hassan's family. She said it would be comforting to the young agent if the president personally presented his condolences and expressed his commiseration; but

Hassan dwelt at the bottom. The president forgot all about him or pretended that he had.

On the eve of the big day aboard the aircraft carrier *Rio de Janeiro*, Felipe Ferraro, after many years without a single sign of anxiety, once more felt the sharp pangs of emotional distress. Again he had that dreadful sense of impending evil.

With that feeling of unease and apprehension, he took a shower before going to bed. When he lay down, Luiza was already asleep. He crossed his arms and stared up at the ceiling. He tried to figure out what could possibly go wrong. He was unable to hit on the slightest idea, so he shut off the light on nightstand and, in the darkness that enclosed him, said a small prayer and asked for reassurance. Then he tried to relax, breathing deeply in and out through the nose in a desperate effort to get rid of that terrible uneasiness.

Suddenly, he heard a violent explosion in the distance. He sat up in bed and listened for other noises, but the only response was silence. Nothing to be heard. For a moment he conjectured on the possible causes. "An Army ammunition dump, maybe," he thought. "No, of course, a gas station. It has to be a gas station… My God, a plane crash! What if it was a plane crash?"

The president jumped out of bed, put on his robe, and left the bedroom. He groped his way through the darkness and sat in a large, comfortable, well-upholstered chair near his desk. He reached for the phone, but backed away. "If it was something serious, they will let me know," he reasoned. "I'm the president for crying out loud!"

He just sat there, dosing off until dawn.

At five thirty, Luiza woke up and went looking for him. She found her husband all dressed up, having breakfast.

"What happened? Why are you up this early?"

Felipe wiped his lips with a napkin, feigning unconcern.

"Nothing, Pookie!" he said, kissing the tip of her nose. "I didn't sleep well last night. I guess this agreement thing has finally caught up with me. You know, all the excitement, the expectations, the whole shebang.

Luiza sat down next to him.

After breakfast he gave her another kiss before she went into the shower. The telephone rang. It was a member of his staff to let him in on the story behind last night's explosion, involving the loss of lives of several policemen and one terrorist. "I want to know all about this in detail when I get back from Rio. Have them write out a complete report, including the background, the works," he said into the mouthpiece before hanging up.

He felt relieved as he walked towards the helicopter that was sitting on the helipad behind the presidential residence, which would ferry him over to the airbase where his plane was waiting. "So that was it, hah!" he mused. "All that fretting on account of the explosion of some rundown hotel way out in the sticks. So what? How can this affect me personally? Well, it won't hurt to look into it when I get back. One step at a time, though. Let's not put the cart before the horse."

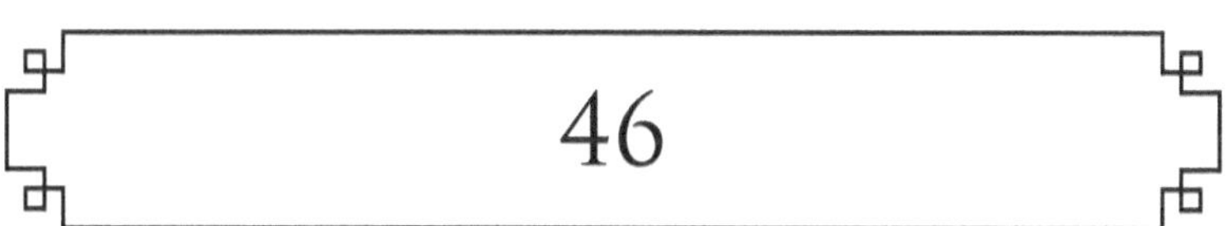

46

The last man of Felipe Ferraro's entourage boarded the presidential plane at exactly five minutes before seven on that sunny morning in Brasilia. The aircraft began to taxi on to the head of the main runway at seven on the dot. It turned around toward the direction from which the wind was blowing, revved to full bore, and headed for takeoff. Gaining altitude, it veered smoothly to the right and glided over across the city.

From his window seat Ibrahim Hassan could glimpse the Metropolitan Cathedral of Our Lady Aparecida and the executive, judicial, and legislative buildings around the Square of Three Powers: Congress, Planalto Presidential Palace, and the Supreme Court. Far off in the distance, lonely and majestic, was the presidential residence, Palacio da Alvorada, or Palace of the Dawn.

Upon steadying on the course to Rio de Janeiro, the huge metal bird climbed up to 30,000 feet.

As he sank into his seat, Hassan discreetly slid his hand under the his armpit and patted the bomb attached to the special holster, just to make sure it was still there.

Drifting into reverie, thoughts dashed through his head, bringing back recent happenings and setting him out on the forthcoming journey into eternity in Paradise for his long-yearned tryst with Raissa. The task that he would have to undertake between now and then was a small, trivial detail: at a certain point during the ceremony all he had to do was to pull that pin firmly and the bomb would explode, killing off the infidels. Of course, he, too, would perish in the process, but his spirit, endowed with glory and honor, would ascend the heavens. As a reward, Allah Himself would cast him into the arms of his cherished, beloved Raissa.

In the seats around Hassan, his colleagues were discussing the flash news on TV about the fire that had burned part of the Bajara Hotel down to a crisp. Apparently the cause was a powerful bomb set off by a terrorist. He had blown himself up and taken several policemen with him.

Nothing had yet been printed in the newspapers. There had been no time. When the tragedy took place, the morning editions were already out and being loaded up into the delivery vans.

Hassan could hear the other agents' chatter, but it did not faze him any. He was totally immersed in his own musing. That lively conversation sounded like idle babbling to him.

In the reserved fore part of the cabin, President Felipe Ferraro and his chief of protocol, Ambassador Carlos Lucena, reviewed the sketch showing the layout of heads of state and guests on the flight deck of the aircraft carrier.

Felipe put the reading glasses back in his pocket. He was happy with the ambassador's clarification.

"So there it is!" he said. "Our guests: Russia, Mexico, United States, Canada, Venezuela, Norway, and Nigeria, in that order, right?"

"Precisely, Mr. President! Eight countries, including ourselves. It's a different kind of G8," the chief of protocol jested with an allusion to the group of nations formed by the seven major economies and Russia.

"It's a shame!" the president sighed. "I wish Saudi Arabia, China, Arab Emirates, well, you know… In short, the major producers would be there."

"I agree, Mr. President! Unfortunately they don't cotton to this idea at all."

"Well, we've come a long way anyhow. I guess we can be optimistic. After all, we have representatives from four different continents."

The ambassador smiled.

"After the luncheon on board the ship," the president said, "I'll go with them to the flight deck for the farewell formalities. They'll be flown by Navy choppers over to the Air Force base where their planes will be waiting, except for President Brian. He brought his own helicopter. I understand none of the presidents is willing to spend an extra day in Brazil?"

"Nobody, Mr. President," said the ambassador. "They're sticking to the approved program."

"Fine by me," the president retorted. "After they're gone, we push off ourselves. I want to go back to Brasilia before this day is out. By the way, what do you know about that hotel that was blown up last night with so many casualties?"

"All I know is what I saw early this morning on the tube, sir."

"I didn't have a chance to see it. Fanzine told me what had happened. I asked him to get the whole factual story. I intend to go to the bottom of this. I'm flabbergasted. Imagine, a terrorist in Brasilia? How crazy is that?

"TV said he hailed from the Middle East," said the ambassador.

"Puzzling! Downright puzzling!"

"And the worst part, Mr. President, was the terrible loss of precious lives. We're talking twenty-two officers killed and five wounded, some of them with very serious injuries."

"There's something very fishy here. I've never heard of any sign of terrorism in Brazil, much less Brasilia. The Feds keep me informed about some sort of investigation on the Triple Frontier requested by the CIA. Nobody was found. Nothing was found"

"Will there be anything else for the moment, Mr. President?"

"No, thank you."

Meanwhile, further back, in another section of the coach cabin, Agent Homero approached Colonel Blake.

"Sir, may I have a word with you?"

Blake raised his head from the notebook.

"Sure thing. Take a load off!" he said gesturing to the empty seat next to him.

"Are you fully informed about that explosion last night?"

"I think so. Why?"

"The terrorist shown on the TV news was a martial arts instructor in wrestling at the gym where Hassan works out."

"Yeah! I knew that. And your point is..."

"Hassan was one of his trainees."

"Does that bother you?

"Well, no, sir, I guess not, but I thought it would be a good idea to let you know." "OK. Thanks!"

To his chagrin the colonel's reaction was not what Homero had expected.

"Beg your pardon, sir," he said and hurried back to his seat.

Shortly after, the president sent for Blake.

The explosion was one of the topics of their conversation. Blake told the president that the dead terrorist was the wrestling instructor of one of his bodyguards. Just a coincidence, to be sure. The colonel reaffirmed his confidence in Agent Hassan, a righteous, morally upright, decent, dedicated young man. "I have a trusting relationship with Hassan, Mr. President."

Back in his seat, Blake summoned Hassan.

"What do you know about that explosion set off by your gym personal trainer?"

"I heard about it, sir. I don't understand all this talk that he was a terrorist, though."

"What do you mean you don't understand?"

"Never figured him for a terrorist, sir, not by a long shot."

"Well, that's not easy to do. Didn't you ever suspect anything?"

"No, sir. He coached a lot of people. Nobody noticed anything wrong with him. Quite the opposite, I should say."

"Did you make friends with him?"

Hassan broke out in one of his rare smiles.

"No, sir," he lied. "I'm not big at making friends, sir, as you know. I go to the gym, change in the locker room, practice on the tatami, and get the hell out. I knew nothing about him, but I can assure you I am quite taken aback by this whole thing."

"Like I said, it's not easy to see through these things. But I believe you, of course. Thanks!"

Hassan sank back into his seat by the window. He did his best to conceal the effects of his self-consciousness. "Now I see how Gamal knew so much about explosives," he reflected. "He was a freaking terrorist. Well, it doesn't matter. It changes nothing and I sure as hell will carry on as planned." He reclined his seat so that he could nap more comfortably and dream of Paradise with Raissa.

47

Before landing at the air base in Rio de Janeiro, the president's plane crisscrossed over the bay. The president wanted to have a bird's eye view of the venue. The *Rio de Janeiro* was laying at anchor off Villegagnon Island, which is home to the Naval Academy.

It was a typical ravishing, sunny day. The 90-foot high statue of Christ the Redeemer, with His open arms, was in full view, standing in its 700-ton frame on top of Corcovado Mountain overlooking the city. At the mouth of the bay, Sugar Loaf Mountain could also be taken in from the plane. The City of Wonder was at its best, with crystal clear blue skies and warm weather; a very beautiful place indeed. Felipe noticed that the majestic carrier had a screen of other warships all around it.

At the end of the tour, the aircraft began the procedure for landing. Approximately two nautical miles abeam of the runway, it went down to 600 feet, extending gear and flaps.

The pilot started a continuous descent, turning 180° back to the runway, maintaining 140 mph throughout the turn. He worked throttle and elevators to be 110 mph over the runway threshold; then he reduced throttle and gradually pulled back on the stick to flair to a smooth touchdown at about 100 mph. The plane taxied gently to its assigned space and came to a full stop.

Exiting through the front door, the president greeted the authorities and shook hands all around. Then he boarded the helicopter with his chief of protocol, aide-de-camp, and security agents. Thirteen minutes later they were landing on the carrier.

The president was rendered the honors prescribed for an official visit to the flagship. The crew was uniformly spaced at the rail of each weather deck, facing outboard. "Attention" was sounded as the president's helicopter approached the ship. As the president set foot on the flight deck, his flag was broken on the yardarm, where it would fly for the duration of the visit. The president was piped aboard, and all military personnel on the flight deck saluted as the honor guard presented arms until the termination of the band's ruffles and the pipe flourishes.

After the usual greetings and formalities, the president, sided by the fleet commander and the captain, lined up to welcome aboard the foreign dignitaries.

Every five minutes a Navy chopper landed, bringing in the exalted guests and their retinues. The U.S. president arrived on a U.S. Air Force helicopter.

A table had been set up near a bulkhead and cordoned off to the other guests and credentialed reporters who stood thirty feet away.

Some senior officials of the president's staff had brought their families. Coincidentally, it was Lt. Col. William Blake's birthday, so he, too, decided to bring his family, since he had intended to stay in Rio de Janeiro until Sunday. Agent Carlos would stand by for him during the president's trip back to Brasilia. Unfortunately, owing to the explosion of the Bajara Hotel, Blake was forced to change his plans. He told Carlos that he would go back with the president after all.

As the other heads of government were arriving, they were escorted to their seats by officers of the ship. Behind them stood the security agents.

Following a discreet gesture from the head of protocol, President Felipe Ferraro began a speech reeking of optimism.

As the president spoke, Hassan, ever so subtle, made a barely perceptible move towards the U.S. secret agent who was closer to the President of the United States. Two seconds before the bomb went off he planned to dart out from the line of onlooking agents and throw himself on President Brian's back, holding on tightly to him in a deadly embrace.

Standing at Hassan's right, Colonel Blake was motionless. His eyes were fixed on the small knot of guests in front of him about 30 feet away from the table, attentive to any suspicious sign.

As he closed his address, President Felipe Ferraro was applauded and cheered by the ceremony's attendees.

A diplomat came forward holding a document with both hands which he placed in front of Felipe. The president signed it. The same diplomat picked it up and gave it to the President of Venezuela, the first country to adhere to the agreement. Next he took it to President Brian.

This was Hassan's self-established cue that he had decided to use to prompt his deadly performance. At that very instant, without hesitation, he reached for the holster, firmly pulled the pin, and began the countdown in his mind. "Tic 50, tic 49, tic 48, tic 43…" And he stopped cold at the sight of a little boy running towards him with his arms open, crying out his name.

"My God, it's Guto!" he managed to mutter in a paroxysm of terror, finally realizing the full meaning of the word.

"Baba! Baba!" Guto cried, while the bomb was ticking very close to Hassan's heart.

"No, Guto, no! Stay back!" Hassan shouted at the top of his lungs.

Hassan leaped over the conference table and, like a sprinter, dashed off towards the edge of the flight deck on the starboard side which was nearer. He jumped overboard.

There was an explosion that sent up a huge splash.

It all happened very quickly, and everybody was frozen on their spots, nobody saying anything. All eyes were on Guto who was running after Hassan before his father caught up with him and gave him to Leticia. There was no reaction on the part of anybody else, until the explosion was heard.

Then all hell broke loose.

The American secret agents, who had already drawn their weapons and surrounded their president, started escorting him back to the helicopter as fast as they could. The other security details followed suit, but the agents didn't know where to point their guns.

The general commotion began to quiet down when Colonel Blake yelled in English, Spanish and Portuguese, urging everyone to keep calm and saying that the situation was under control.

In his mother's arms, Guto, just a little boy barely over three years old, did not know that he had saved the day along with the lives of seven presidents thus preventing a disaster of unpredictable consequences. The strong security apparatus and display of power had proved absolutely useless.

The immense love for that child burst forth into a thousand flames that healed Hassan's hate-hardened heart. That love shone so overwhelmingly when he saw the boy that, in a split second, its blinding light blotted out the evil that lurked in his frenzied desire for revenge.

Guto was an all-powerful instrument of divine intervention.

247

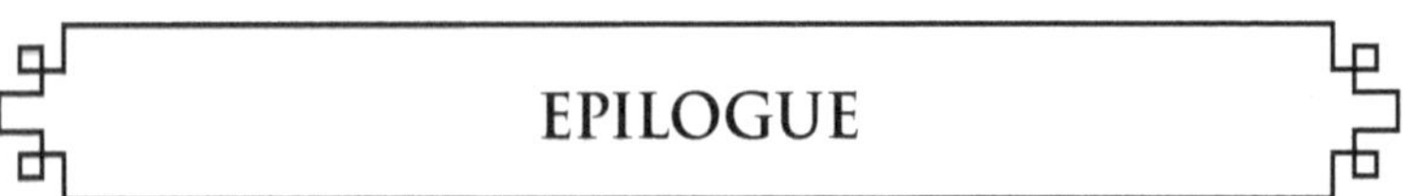

EPILOGUE

A crime is configured only when there is evidence that the law has been broken; thus the need for an inquiry.

Upon request from the Interpol in Brazil, Portuguese detective Mauricio Santana was assigned to join the investigation into Gamal's criminal activities in Portugal and Brazil. Raquel, albeit her arm in a sling, was also part of the team whose job was to trace Gamal Abdul's steps backwards from the Bajara Hotel in Brasilia to that hostel at Bairro da Graça in Lisbon.

Testimony from depositions of a large number of witnesses was central throughout the investigation.

A link was found between the terrorist and the president's bodyguard Ibrahim Hassan. It was established that they met at the mosque, but nothing was ever discovered about the refuge, because Sergeant Deivid, the only witness to its existence, was dead.

After a thorough, systematic examination, the police were led to the suspicion that both the sergeant and the watchman had been murdered by Gamal, but lack of concrete evidence prevented confirmation. They never found a single trace of Soraia or any clue to the identities and whereabouts of the other two terrorists.

The case of the double murder of Jandira and her lover was quickly and duly closed. The statements of the flannel boy Antonio Serafim supported by Clovis, the drycleaner, cleared up the mystery, and there was no doubt that the late detective Marcelo Moreira was the culprit. The broker Sergio Gomes was set free, and he successfully sued the City on several counts.

Vitoria Bajara, counseled by Ilse Ancora, attorney-at-law and Nice's cousin, filed suit for a couple of million *reais* and won. Nice was a great help to Vitoria during the hotel's restoration. Neide sued Vitoria and lost. Advised by Ilse, Vitoria left everything she owned to Nice in her will.

Policewoman Raquel Lopes, inasmuch as she had been disabled in the line of duty, was given an early retirement with full pay.

Raquel and Mauricio were highly praised for a job well done.

They were married in Lisbon, and today they live in a cozy, spacious apartment on the lovely beach of Cascais in Lisbon.

Raquel is with child. It's a girl.

Lisbon/ Rio de Janeiro, February, 2009.

A NOTE ON THE AUTHOR

TARCIZO SOBREIRA FERNANDES is a retired Brazilian Navy captain and a fiction writer.

WORKS PUBLISHED include articles, short stories, chronicles published in newspapers and magazines, and TV sketches.

In Brazil

- *A Sailor*– chronicles and poems, ©1984
- *The Network*– a crime novel, ©1989
- *A Treason for a Treason*– a crime novel, ©1996

In Portugal

- *Mister President*– a crime novel, ©2007

www.ingramcontent.com/pod-product-compliance
Lightning Source LLC
Chambersburg PA
CBHW032242310726

48973CB00008B/2251